THE ENDING SERIES

WORLD BEFORE

LINDSEY POGUE   LINDSEY FAIRLEIGH

World Before
by Lindsey Fairleigh and Lindsey Pogue

Editing by Sarah Kolb-Williams
www.kolbwilliams.com

Cover Design by Deranged Doctor Designs

L2 Books
101 W American Canyon Rd. Ste. 508 – 262
American Canyon, CA 94503

978-1-949485-05-9

FOREWORD

AN EXCERPT FROM THE JOURNAL OF ZOE CARTWRIGHT

MAY 22, 1AE

Looking backward at the past and then forward to the future, I think about how changeable life is. How two years ago I feared such trivial things, like being unable to pay my rent on time or make a car payment. Now, along with hoping for the future, I fear what I don't know—there's still so much left to learn about this new world we're living in. In many ways, I fear my Ability, because there's still so much to learn about the people around me, too.

Abilities are interesting things. They scared the shit out of us before we understood what they were and learned to embrace them; now, we depend on them to keep us together and to keep us safe. My dad can alter the memories and perceptions of others to protect and benefit our family; Dani's telepathy allows her to communicate with people and use animals as scouts; Jason can nullify other Abilities; Jake can regenerate physically, allowing him to take more risks than any of us; Gabe can communicate through dreams; Becca and Harper can see possible futures—the list goes on and on, and all the benefits our Abilities bring have strengthened us. They are a big part of what's kept us alive in this often-crazy world. Most of us, anyway. Many of our friends fought long and hard but didn't survive in the end, though we think about them all the time—Dave, Ben, Sarah, Tavis, my mom...

But it's Ky I think about the most.

Ky was one of the soldiers who helped Jason find Dani, back when this all started. He was a jokester and a friend, and he helped keep an eye on my best friend while we were still trying to find one another during year one. Ky was also an empath, like me. He could feel what others were feeling, and alongside the others, I watched his Ability to sense every emotion the others felt—good and bad—consume him. Granted, those were the darker months in the beginning, when we were lost and cold; we didn't know what we do now. We were scared and alone and searching for comfort in a world that offered us none, and that took those we loved away from us for a little added punch. So yes, in those months, Ky was consumed and debilitated by his empathic Ability. I worry that might happen to me one day, too.

Like Ky, I can feel what people are feeling, but I can also see their memories of their lives before and sense the essence of who they are in their auras. Despite how well-honed my Ability is now and how well I can control it, I've learned things over the months that I shouldn't know. I've seen into people's minds; I know their darkest secrets, the most painful parts of their pasts. What haunts them sometimes haunts me, and there is no one I can tell. I'm the keeper of secrets, it would seem.

Memories. Feelings. Truths. This is my power. The unspoken agreement between myself and those closest to me is this: just keep it to yourself. And I do, mostly. Sometimes, the memories I see strike a chord not easily ignored. There are some memories, no matter how damning or intimate, that need to be told. Stories that shed a much-needed light on the past. Facts that seem important, even if I can't tell anyone what they are. Truths that remind us how gray life can be, that there is no black or white or bad or good in this world. That there never has been.

FOREWORD

I found this journal in an old bag of my things in my closet. I started writing in it when I lost my memory last year, back when I was me but didn't know who me *was, when I was desperate to understand who people were and how they fit into my life. So I wrote about them in here, trying to make sense of things. It tends to get a little hectic around here from time to time, so after a while, I stopped writing. Until now. A weight lifted from my shoulders the second I laid eyes on it. I can't tell anyone what's in my mind—about all of the things I see—but I* can *continue to write them down.*

So that's what this journal is for—a place of safekeeping for the memories that might one day, years from now, come to mean something to more people than myself. Stories of how everything began and how things were for us before The Ending.

I

April 27, 1 AE

I have no idea what I was planning on using this journal for before I lost my memory, but now, it's the only place I can be myself, not judged by listening ears. Everyone expects old me, but all I can give them is new me instead. I hate the looks of disappointment on their faces. It only makes me feel worse. I wish they knew how it feels to not know who you are but to be expected to act like it anyway. The old me would probably love them for missing me so much and wishing I were back to normal, and I try to be understanding. In fact, I think I'm doing a pretty damn good job of it, but it's hard sometimes. Gabe gets it, I think.

He rode with me on the cart today, said he had a way for me to get my old-Zoe-self back again, or at least an idea of how to. As exciting as the idea is, it's what I learned about Gabe during our awkward ride on the cart that has stuck with me. He flat-out requested that I keep whatever memories of his I see to myself, so I will...but that doesn't mean I can't write them down, right? It's not like I'll be sharing this with anyone.

And anyway, if the day comes when I'm old Zoe again, I feel like I might want to know these things, especially if Gabe and I are friends, and if I'm with Jake...and especially if Jake and Gabe have such a troubled past. Geez, a girl could get lost in all of this, so I hope this glimpse of them from before will be helpful—to both old and new me.

"Hey, Gabe," the girl called from across the living room, crooking her finger to beckon him closer. She pouted her bottom lip and turned her red plastic cup upside down. "I'm empty, and I'm oh so thirsty, but I don't know how to make the keg work." She was come-hithering pretty hard. "Come help me."

The girl was Chelsea Hawkins, a smoking-hot junior at Gabe's high school with a reputation for flirting but not following through. Gabe should've been honored that she'd even made an appearance at he and Jake's party. He should've been crawling toward her on hands and knees, begging for whatever attention she deigned worthy of a lowly sophomore like himself. But there were so many other girls around who posed far less of a challenge, and Gabe hadn't risked being grounded for the rest of his life by throwing this party during his parents' annual January Hawaii trip to simply follow Chelsea Hawkins around like a lost puppy all night.

"I'm sure you can figure it out," Gabe said, then returned his attention to the girl sitting beside him on the windowsill. He couldn't remember her name—she went to a different school, and he'd only just met her—but she sure was cute. And with the way she was making eyes at him, she wouldn't be much of a challenge at all. He glanced at Chelsea, not surprised to see that some other guy had swooped in to save the day. Specifically, Jake, Gabe's live-in best friend and all-around nice guy. He and his sister, Becca, had been living with Gabe's family for the past year or two, and Gabe knew him well enough to guess that he probably had zero ulterior motives and genuinely wanted to help Chelsea. *Sucker,* Gabe thought, smirking.

"She's, like, really pretty," the girl on the windowsill said, biting her lip. A tiny crease appeared between her eyebrows, which Gabe found adorable.

"*You're* really pretty," he told her. Girls liked hearing that kind of thing, and he figured it was true enough. He leaned down to brush a lock of hair out of her face, tucking it behind her ear. "What do you say we go somewhere a little more private?"

The girl blushed, averting her eyes to the floor, and nodded. "Sure," she said, gazing up at him through her lashes. "I'd like that."

Gabe grinned, hoping he didn't look too eager, and took her hand in his. He led her to the stairs, but he paused with his foot on the second step. Lizzie, his kid sister, stood at the top of the staircase in her usual sleepwear of an oversized t-shirt, pale as a ghost and clutching her chest. She was breathing hard, practically panting. Becca, Jake's little sister, stood beside her, an arm wrapped around her waist.

"Lizzie?" Gabe released his prize's hand and jogged up the stairs, stopping a couple steps from the top so he was at eye level with his sister. She was not quite four years his junior, but she'd always been small for her age. He placed his hands on her shoulders and searched her face for signs of what was wrong. "Did you have a bad dream?"

Lizzie shook her head, her expression pained. And afraid. "I can't breathe, Gabe." She gripped his arm with one hand, the other scratching at her chest. "I can't…" A bead of crimson appeared in her right nostril, streaking down over her lips and dripping onto the carpet.

"Lizzie, your nose—"

Her eyes rolled back into her head, and her knees gave out. Becca's hold on her waist wasn't nearly strong enough to keep her upright.

Gabe caught Lizzie before she tumbled down the stairs, scooping her up and hurrying to the ground floor. He barely felt his sister's weight in his arms; all he could think about was getting help. "Jake!" He raced into the kitchen, backing through the swinging door.

Jake was standing at the keg with Chelsea, midway through explaining how the thing worked. He looked at Gabe, eyebrows raised. When Jake saw that Gabe was carrying Lizzie, he abandoned his damsel in distress and rushed toward his friend. "What happened?"

"She just collapsed," Becca said from behind Gabe. "We were telling ghost stories in our room, and she started having a hard time breathing, and—"

"I need your car, man," Gabe interrupted. "I gotta get her to the hospital." The Colorado Springs Medical Center was only four blocks away; driving her himself would be faster than going through the song and dance of calling 9-1-1.

Gabe sat with his sister in the back seat while Jake drove, Becca riding up front with her brother. It only took a few minutes to get to the hospital, but it felt like hours. Jake brought the car to a stop right in front of the sliding emergency room doors and Gabe jumped out, pulling his unconscious little sister out of the car after him. Cradling her limp body in his arms, he hurried into the emergency room.

The minutes, hours, days after passed in a blur. The diagnosis—leukemia—bounced around inside Gabe, like his entire body was hollow. The prognosis—a year, maybe—left him numb.

Lizzie was just a kid. She was only in seventh grade. She'd barely lived at all, and now she was sick because something in her DNA had gone haywire. She hadn't done anything to deserve this. It should've been Gabe who was sick. Who was dying. He was the one who broke all the rules. The one who only cared about school because it was where all the girls went during the day. It should've been him, not Lizzie.

It wasn't fair.

"I can't believe you're pussing out, man," Kevin, his friend—or former friend—scoffed. "You used to be fun, but now you're just…" He made an ugly face and shook his head, then stomped away, kicking a chair as he left the cafeteria.

Gabe could feel Jake's eyes on his face. "I'm fine." It had been six months since that fateful night in the emergency room, and Gabe's life had been consumed by the need to help the doctors find a way to save his sister. So long as everyone would leave him the hell alone, he'd be just fine, damn it.

Jake grunted. "When do you leave for camp?"

Tearing his focus from the medical journal he'd been reading, Gabe looked across the round table at his best friend. Possibly his only friend, now. "Why do you have to make it sound like some pussified sleep-away camp? It's a summer program. On biology. At a university. I'll be staying in a dorm room, not a shitty cabin, and I'll spend all my time learning about genetics, not sitting around campfires, singing songs and eating s'mores."

"Campfires and s'mores...that doesn't sound so bad."

Gabe raised an eyebrow. "You want to hold hands and sing 'Kumbaya'?"

"Yeah," Jake said, deadpan. "It's my life's goal. Duh."

Gabe almost smiled, which was saying a lot.

"Let's go camping before you leave." A hint of concern touched Jake's eyes. "It'll be good for you to take a break. Clear your head."

"I can't, man," Gabe said, shaking his head. "I gotta keep—"

"What? Trying to one-up the doctors?"

Gabe closed his mouth, his eyes narrowing.

But Jake didn't back down. "Take a break. Come camping. Take time to process all this shit you've been shoving into your head. Maybe then you really will come up with some brilliant cure the doctors missed."

Gabe held Jake's stare for a moment longer, then shrugged,

looking back down at the article he'd been reading. "Fine, whatever."

Gabe stood in the hallway, staring into the hospital room with the odd sense that he wasn't really there. That this wasn't really happening. He'd just been at school, trying not to nod off during Junior English, barely an hour ago. And now…

The incessant screeching and beeping from the machines screaming warnings about his sister's vital signs faded away, replaced by a dull roar within his skull. A thumping. A *whoosh whoosh whoosh.*

The people rushing around in the room, all wearing scrubs, seemed to be moving in slow motion as they attempted to revive Lizzie. Her body jerked at the jolt of electricity from a defibrillator.

Gabe backed away, feeling like he was floating. Dazedly, he found his way to the men's room down the hall. He stood in front of a sink and turned on the cold water, intending to splash it on his face. Instead, he leaned over, gripping porcelain, and vomited.

He watched the sickly mixture of bile and coffee slip down the drain, then tugged a paper towel from the dispenser and wiped his mouth.

With a creak and a squeak, the bathroom door opened, and Jake walked in. He leaned his shoulder against the wall, hands tucked into his jeans pockets, but didn't say anything.

Gabe looked at him in the mirror, then stared at his own reflection. He didn't recognize himself, like he was in somebody else's body. Like this was somebody else's life. Like he'd just watched somebody else's sister die.

"Is this really happening?" he asked, voice hoarse. It felt like a dream. A nightmare. He blinked. His eyes felt scratchy. "I'd like to wake up now."

"They said you can sit with Lizzie until your parents get here." His dad had a business trip in Chicago, and his mom had joined him, because the doctors had all said Lizzie was stable for the time being. Liars.

"Lizzie." Gabe looked at Jake in the mirror once more. "But she—she's not there. She's not…" He shook his head slowly, at a loss for words.

Jake bowed his head. "I know, man." He pushed off the wall, stepping further into the bathroom, and placed a hand on Gabe's shoulder. "I know."

Gabe made a choking sound, hunching in on himself.

All the afternoons spent doing homework at Lizzie's bedside while she slept. All the evenings spent reading to her because she was too weak to hold up a book herself. All the trips out to her favorite fast-food restaurants to pick up treats he'd have to sneak past the nurses. What was he going to do with his time now? This had become his life. Lizzie had taken over his world.

And now she was gone.

They still had one more Harry Potter book to get through. She'd never find out what happened.

Because she was gone.

It was over for her.

But for Gabe, it was only just beginning.

"Hey, man," Gabe said, bursting into Jake's room, "it came."

Jake was lying on his back on his bed, eyes closed and headphones blaring.

Gabe tapped Jake's nose with the edge of the envelope that would decide his fate, one way or the other.

Jake's eyes popped open, and he moved one headphone away from his ear.

"Stanford," Gabe said, waving the envelope over Jake's face. He'd been waiting for the envelope to come for months.

Eyebrows raised, Jake sat up, pulling the headphones down so they hung around his neck. "It's small," he said, looking from the envelope to Gabe and back.

"I know," Gabe said. "I think that means I didn't get in. That's what everyone says, at least." He held the envelope out to Jake. "Open it. Give me the bad news. I can't do it myself."

Jake inhaled and exhaled deeply, then took the envelope.

Gabe turned away, rubbing the back of his neck and pacing around the bed. The sound of paper ripping made his heart race. He licked his lips. "Well?"

"Holy shit, man."

Gabe stopped at the foot of the bed and faced Jake. "What? What does it say?"

"You—you got in." Jake's eyes skimmed the letter. "Gabe, you more than got in. They're offering you a *full ride*."

Gabe's lips spread into an uncertain smile before he'd fully processed the words that had come out of Jake's mouth. He stumbled forward and sat on the bed, tearing the acceptance letter from Jake's grip and laughing breathily. He couldn't believe it until he saw the words with his own two eyes. And there they were, right in front of his face. "Holy shit." That unsure smile turned into a full-on grin. "Holy fucking shit."

Stanford had the best post-bac genetics program in the country, and excelling there as an undergrad would almost guarantee Gabe a spot in that elite graduate program in a few years. If he didn't have to worry about working to help pay the way as an undergrad, then he'd have all the time in the world for his studies. He'd finally have the knowledge and resources to go to war with the thing that had taken his sister from him.

And, damn it, he would win.

Sitting at his desk in the office he shared with Carly, another PhD student, Gabe flipped open the latest copy of the *New England Journal of Medicine*. His article was on page eighteen, explaining his breakthrough study using gene therapy to battle acute lymphocytic leukemia. The treatment had proven a groundbreaking 97 percent success rate with the dogs used during the second phase of testing, and he was just awaiting approval from the FDA to begin clinical trials on humans.

He combed his fingers through his hair and, for a moment, thought of his mother back in Colorado Springs. She'd be nagging him to cut his hair—it was almost long enough to tie back in a ponytail—but he just couldn't seem to find the time. His research was everything to him, and it took up every minute of every day.

His mother would understand his devotion to his work, at least. She still mourned Lizzie's death almost as if it just happened. For a while there, during the first couple years, Gabe hadn't been sure his mom would pull through; her broken heart weakened her, and she struggled with depression as well as a string of illnesses. But Gabe's ceaseless focus and determination to battle the thing that had taken Lizzie's life, to find a cure for the incurable, helped his mother pull through.

The phone rang.

Gabe set down the medical journal, reached for the receiver, and brought it up to his ear, leaning back in his chair. "Gabriel McLaughlin," he said absently. It was probably one of his lab minions calling in sick. It happened more often than Gabe would like, but then, he drove them pretty hard.

"Yes, hello, Gabriel," a woman said. "My name is Anna Wesley, and I'm—"

Gabe straightened in his chair, hinges squeaking. "Dr. Anna Wesley? *The* Dr. Anna Wesley?"

The woman chuckled on the other end of the line. "Yes, that's correct."

"Holy shit. I mean…" Gabe ran his fingers through his hair. "Excuse the profanity, ma'am, but you're a legend."

"Am I?" She let out a dry laugh. "Well, at least there's that."

Now that his knee-jerk reaction was out of the way, Gabe was utterly speechless.

"Gabriel, I'm calling to offer you a position working on my team at—"

"Yes," Gabe said, finding enough of his voice to utter that single word.

"But you don't even know what the job is," Dr. Wesley said, humor tinting her tone.

It didn't matter. Gabe had learned all he could from his professors at Stanford, and his PhD was all but granted. In a few weeks, he'd be out of there, hunting for the perfect, well-funded lab to call home. Dr. Wesley's lab would be ideal. Working with her was a once-in-a-lifetime opportunity. He couldn't pass it up.

However, Gabe didn't want to seem overeager. "Good point," he said, clearing his throat. "What can you tell me about the position?"

Dr. Wesley was quiet for a moment. "Well, it's for the Department of Defense. You'd have to relocate to Colorado Springs."

"Colorado Springs?" Gabe repeated back to her, narrowing his eyes in thought. That wouldn't be a problem, considering his mom still lived there and Jake and Becca had just bought a house there.

But where in Colorado Springs did the DOD have any kind of research lab set up? Something nagged at him from the far recesses of his mind. He'd seen a few journal articles over the years come out of an Air Force university in his hometown. It was on the tip of his tongue—something with a *P*. Suddenly, the image of a highway exit sign surfaced in his mind, and he knew what it was.

"Would that be Peterson Air Force Base?" he asked.

"Why yes," Dr. Wesley said, "yes, it would."

2

May 24, 1 AE

It's funny how much time can pass in the flip of a page. Although it was only a month ago that I started this journal, I'd completely forgotten about it until now. A lot has changed since I last wrote in here—it seems like an entire lifetime, actually. I have my memory back now. So, yay! It was all thanks to Gabe, Chris, and my mom. I've had it back for a while now, and it's those lingering memories that once again draw me to this book's blank pages, prepared to write until my fingers hurt. I don't mind writing, though. It's therapeutic, and I still think this is a really helpful way to get some of these thoughts out of my head, especially the overwhelming ones.

Today, a group of us rode to what was once Bodega Bay. We've been chatting about settling down somewhere, and even though no one has come right out and said it yet, I know they are thinking of settling here. When I say "they," I mean Dani and Jason and Mr. G. I'm not sure how I feel about that prospect, other than that it hurts to think about. The old, painful memories from my childhood are stronger here, and I'm not sure I want to go back. Not with Dad and Grams gone, leaving only the hurtful memories of before behind.

As we walked along the fenced-in town today, I could barely believe my eyes—everything has changed. The town has been sectioned off, farms are cropping up on the side of the road, boats are being repurposed, and ad-hoc committees are running what's now called New Bodega.

I know this is where Dani and Jason first ran into Mr. Grayson, and I've seen it in his memories time and time again, so I wasn't surprised by what I saw as much as I was struck by what I felt. It still feels like home, but also like a new place at the same time. It's just another reminder of how different things are and how quickly we've adapted, Mr. Grayson at the survivalist helm, at least for now.

Honestly, after high school, I was happy to never see any of my teachers again. I hadn't given Mr. G a thought one way or the other, but when I learned that he'd survived, when I saw him with his mountain-man beard back in Colorado, I was grateful to have him back in my life. He's been settling into our group of misfit survivors, but it was today in town when I saw him shine for the first time. He was in his element, and he had a sense of purpose I hadn't realized he'd been longing for.

When Bethany mentioned how Grams's skills would be very handy in a world like this, I noticed Mr. G's eyes flash with a remorse I hadn't been expecting. I couldn't help it; I was too curious, and I opened my mind to his. The memory I saw reminded me what our lives were like before so acutely that it made my eyes sting with tears. Of course, I told Dani it was the wind, and maybe it was, at least a little, but had I not been on my horse, I might've given Mr. G a great big hug and told him how much I love him for who he is and all he's done for me.

Daniel leaned against the table and surveyed the attendees sitting in the classroom, waiting for his final presentation. Parent-teacher night was a simple affair at Bodega Bay High School—the parents, many accompanied by their kids, went through a shortened version of their children's daily class schedules, attending a half dozen ten-minute "classes" over a two-hour period. The bell was about to ring and announce the beginning of this evening's abbreviated sixth period.

Almost all of the seats were filled by parents and students from Daniel's AP American Government class, though one seat remained empty. Zoe Cartwright sat beside Dani O'Connor—no surprise there, the two were practically joined at the hip—and Dani's grandmother, Ceara, was seated beside her granddaughter, just as she'd been during parent-teacher night the previous three years.

Figuring the empty seat beside Zoe was being saved for her one and only parent, Daniel crossed his arms and said, "We'll just wait a moment for any stragglers." Tom, Zoe's father, must've been out using the restroom.

Zoe stared down at her hands, linked together on her lap, neck and cheeks flushed.

After nearly a minute passed without any new arrivals, Daniel cleared his throat and stood. Apparently, Tom wasn't in attendance this evening. "Well then," Daniel said, "let's begin..."

The final session of the night was easy enough. All of the students in his AP American Government class had been his students for three years now, and all of the parents had heard Daniel's spiel about responsibility, accountability, and good old hard work several times over the years he'd taught social studies to their children.

Once the bell rang, concluding the session, he stood in the hall just outside the doorway to his classroom and shook hands with the parents and students alike as they filed out. He felt that same odd sense of apprehension that struck him every year when the parents of seniors shook his hand on parent-teacher night, thanked him, and left his room for the last time. These students he'd watched grow from children to young adults over the past few years would be leaving his classroom for good come spring. Some would remain in Bodega Bay, but most would leave, heading off to start new adventures. Many he would never see again.

"You two go on and get some goodies from the bake sale for me," Ceara said, handing her granddaughter some money before ushering her and Zoe out of the room. Ceara's Irish lilt lent a musicality to her words that made everything she said sound enchanting to Daniel's ears. "I'd like to have a word with Da—Mr. Grayson, just for a moment." When the two teens paused in the doorway, she made a shooing motion. "Go on now."

In Daniel's mind, Ceara O'Connor's status as a grandmother was merely a technicality. She was, for all intents and purposes, Dani's mother, having raised the girl since birth, when her own teenaged mother passed away. Ceara was, so far as the parents of his students went, on the older side, but she was far from elderly. She was a dignified late-sixties, maybe ten years his senior. Her hair was that fine silver-gray that only graced the blessed few, and her emerald-green eyes were bright with the light of an entire lifetime's worth of experiences, both joyous and sad. She was not exactly beautiful, at least to Daniel, but she was striking. And her inner strength and whipcrack wit made her very attractive indeed.

Daniel stepped through the doorway, reentering his classroom, and stuffed his hands into his trouser pockets. "I hope all is well, Ceara," he said, both a statement and a question.

"Oh, yes, well enough," Ceara said with a dismissive wave of her hand. "Please"—she gestured to a pair of chairs tucked behind student desks—"sit with me for a moment. I wish to speak with you." She inhaled and exhaled deeply. "About Zoe."

Daniel frowned, unsure where this was going, and made his way to the proffered chair.

Ceara sat, crossing her ankles, angling her knees toward Daniel, and tucking her feet under the chair. "The poor girl," she said with a heavy sigh and a shake of her head. "She'd never tell you so herself, but her father…he's failing her. Zoe spends most of her time at my house these days—not that I mind having her there, of course, but she is a child of loss, and a blind person would be able to see that both she and her father need each other, especially with Jason off serving the country."

Daniel was quiet for a moment, processing her words. "Well," he started, "I can't say I haven't noticed a change in Zoe. She's withdrawn and subdued, especially when your granddaughter isn't nearby, and her performance in my class has been suffering a little. I thought maybe AP was the wrong track for her, but now…" He leaned a forearm on the desk, nodding as he considered the situation. "I can't say I'm surprised that there's trouble at home. Tom's been through a lot." If Daniel recalled correctly, losing his wife had nearly destroyed Tom all those years ago. "He's come a long way since Anna's death," he said, "and I have to say, Zoe's resemblance to her mother is nothing short of haunting. It must pain him to see what he lost every day when he looks at his daughter."

"Pffft," Ceara said, shaking her head. "You and I both know what it is to lose the person you planned to spend the rest of your life with. 'Tis no excuse. He's not the only one who lost her. Zoe and Jason lost a mother, too, and I dare say they needed her more than he did. And now they—Zoe—*needs* him. She needs him to *be* her father, while he still can." Ceara reached out, placing her fingertips on Daniel's forearm. "He's close to losing her for good, Daniel, and that'll only hurt both of them further."

It was Daniel's turn to sigh. "I'm assuming that because you're here talking to me about this, you think I can help in some way."

With a slight smile, Ceara gave his arm a squeeze, then released it. "I'd have you speak with him. I've tried, but…" She shook her head. "I think I'm too close to the family. My words fall on deaf ears. But you—you're practically a stranger to him, and a widower as well. Hearing this coming from you will be more of a shock…might even knock some sense into him." She paused for a moment. "Besides, I had more time with my Patrick than he had with Anna; I feel like I'm gloating when I speak to Tom of loss. My instincts tell me that you may be able to get through to him where I cannot."

Daniel's shoulders worked their way up to a tense shrug. He wasn't fond of talking about his deceased wife, Michelle, but dredging up the past would be a small price to pay if it meant Zoe and her father could regain some semblance of a healthy relationship. "I suppose it wouldn't hurt to try," he said. At least, it wouldn't hurt anyone but himself.

"Truly, you will?" Ceara said, hand to her chest and smile broad. "It would mean the world to me…and to Zoe, of course."

Daniel gave a hesitant nod, returning her smile with a weak one of his own.

"You're a saint, Daniel Grayson," Ceara said, cupping his cheek gently. "Don't let anyone tell you otherwise."

Daniel looked away, clearing his throat gruffly. Why was it suddenly so warm in the classroom?

Ceara stood and started for the hall. She paused at the doorway and half turned to look back at Daniel. "Zoe has basketball practice tomorrow afternoon, so she won't be home until six or so. I'll meet you here once school's out and the kids have gone."

Daniel opened his mouth, eyebrows raised. "Why would you do that?"

"Oh, aye…you didn't think I'd let you go alone, did you?" Her lips spread into a smile once more, this one soft and warm.

"Well I—I hadn't really thought about it."

Her green eyes sparkled with kindness. "I'll see you tomorrow, Daniel," she said and left the classroom.

Daniel stared at the place where Ceara had stood just moments ago, mind already working on the task ahead. At least, *most* of his mind. A small, secret part was lost to thoughts of the ever-enchanting Ceara O'Connor.

"I haven't been here since Jason's graduation party," Daniel said, staring out through the windshield at the Cartwright family home.

"Oh, yes, I remember it well," Ceara said. "Zoe and my Dani refused to let him graduate without a proper celebration." She smiled to herself, laughing softly. "When Jason announced that he'd already enlisted in the Army…"

"The party definitely took a turn for the…interesting," Daniel said, chuckling uncomfortably. Even the memory of the fight that followed between Jason and his father made Daniel uneasy. This family had been through so much; he felt a renewed desire to do what he could to help out. "Well"—he inhaled deeply, then cleared his throat—"I suppose we should get to it. No time like the present."

Ceara touched his arm. "You're doing the right thing, Daniel. You know that, don't you?"

Looking into her eyes, he nodded.

Once out of the car, they made their way up the front deck to the door. Nobody answered when Daniel knocked, nor when he rang the doorbell.

"He'll be out back in his workshop, then," Ceara said. "Come on. It's this way." She headed down the porch steps and followed a gravel path, disappearing around the corner of the house.

Daniel walked fast to catch up, following her around to the back deck and down the stairs. They crossed the lawn to a large shed, passing an old tire swing hanging from a cypress along the way. Tom, Zoe's father, was visible through the shed's window, bowed over a workbench.

Ceara knocked on the door. Daniel watched Tom through the window, and he didn't move. It was as though he hadn't even heard the knock on the door.

Ceara knocked again, and when there was still no visible response from Tom, she reached for the doorknob and let herself in. She took two steps into the workshop and planted her hands on her hips. "Thomas Cartwright, have you gone deaf, then?"

Tom started, spinning around, chisel in hand. “Wha—”

“We’ve been knocking and knocking…” Daniel imagined Ceara’s eyebrows raised and her mouth pinched, though her face wasn’t visible to him.

“Ceara?” Tom set down the chisel and made his way around the worktable separating them. “What are you doing here? Is Zoe —did something happen?” Panic flashed in his eyes. “Is she—”

Ceara held up one hand, soothing his worry. “Your girl is fine, Tom.” She half turned, gesturing to Daniel. “But she is why we’re here. You remember Daniel Grayson, don’t you?”

Tom stepped around Ceara and stretched out his arm, offering his hand to Daniel. “The history teacher, right?”

Daniel shook Tom’s hand. “That’s me.”

Tom retreated back into the workshop and leaned against the edge of a worktable. “What can I do for you?”

Ceara wandered away, examining the tools scattered along the workbenches all around the shop and the projects in various states of doneness.

“Well, I—” Daniel stepped into the workshop and turned to shut the door. The smell of wood was overwhelming but not unpleasant, accompanied by a hint of some sort of oil and aromatic chemicals. Varnishes and stains and the like, he supposed. “I wanted to check in with you about your daughter’s performance at school.”

Tom frowned. “I don’t understand—Zoe’s always been a good student. Has she done something, or…?”

“No,” Daniel said, shaking his head. “No, nothing like that.” He took a deep breath. “Mr. Cartwright—Tom—last night was parent-teacher night. Did you know about it?”

“Oh…” Tom raised one hand, rubbing his furrowed brow. “I didn’t realize it was last night.” His focus slipped away from Daniel, shifting to the window instead. “Zoe mentioned it a couple times, but I—” He shrugged his shoulders. “I guess I lost track of the days. Zoe usually reminds me of things, but she didn't say anything about it yesterday…"

"She has basketball practice after school, Tom," Ceara reminded him, a hint of scolding in her voice. "She waited for you at the school. She called you."

Tom's shoulders slumped. "No wonder she was so quiet last night." Pain etched lines into his weathered face. It was clear that he cared deeply about his daughter; he was just having a hard time getting that to translate into action.

"Zoe's grades are slipping," Daniel told him. "She's become withdrawn around the other students. She's distracted." He paused for a second, letting that sink in. "Your daughter is struggling in school, Tom, and for most students, that struggle spills over from home."

Tom crossed his arms over his chest, returning his stare to Daniel. "It hasn't been easy around here since her mother…" His gaze slipped back to the window, his jaw tensing. "And now with Jason gone…"

"I know," Daniel said. "I understand. I lost my wife, too, years ago. Complications due to childbirth." He stepped to the side, recapturing Tom's stare. "Our son followed her a day later." Daniel swallowed roughly, his throat suddenly dry. "I know what it feels like to lose the person you love most in the world…to have your future stolen away. But Zoe also lost someone—her mom. Jason left her behind, too. But she's still here, and she still needs you. She needs her father to *be* a father."

A humorless, breathy laugh escaped Tom and his arms fell from his chest to hang limp at his sides. "She takes care of me far better than I take care of her, I know that. I just…" He met Daniel's eyes. "I didn't realize how much this—how much *I'm* hurting her." He shook his head, beseeching with his hands. "What can I do? I don't want to lose her, too."

Relief flooded Daniel. For all appearances, it looked like Ceara's instincts had been right: he, a relative stranger, had managed to get through to Tom. "Well, there's a girls' basketball game tomorrow," Daniel said. "Why don't you start by going and cheering her on?"

Tom nodded to himself. "That's a great idea. Basketball…" He let out a single, breathy laugh. "I didn't even realize the season had started."

Daniel felt a strange combination of irritation and empathy for Zoe's father. On one hand, he understood what it was to lose those closest to you, but on the other hand, he'd learned long ago that moving on wasn't the same thing as letting go. The world had still gone on turning without Michelle in it; the desire to continue living had felt like a betrayal, at first, but Daniel's sister had smacked some sense into him by pointing out that Michelle wouldn't have found it the least bit endearing or romantic for him to give up on life because she was gone. So he'd kept moving forward, going through the motions until he found himself enjoying the ride once more.

"I think it's time for some tea," Ceara said, making a beeline for the door. "We can all have a seat and brainstorm ways to untangle this mess. What do you boys say to that?"

"I'd like to ask you something," Daniel said as he pulled into the parking spot beside Ceara's sedan in the school lot. He put his car in park and turned off the ignition, returning his attention to the stately woman in the passenger seat.

"Oh aye," Ceara said with a kind smile, "go ahead, then."

"Would you—" Daniel cleared his throat and angled his knees toward Ceara. "I don't suppose you'd be interested in going out to dinner…with me. Tomorrow night, perhaps?"

Ceara's smile widened, her emerald eyes sparkling. "I would love to, Daniel, I truly would."

Daniel's brief moment of elation fizzled out as her smile waned. "I'm sensing a 'but' coming."

Ceara sighed. "With my Dani-girl in your class, it just doesn't feel right."

"Oh," Daniel said, gaze sliding to the windshield. A student—a freshman in his fourth-period World Civilizations class—passed by on the sidewalk ahead, oblivious to the grown man getting his heart broken just a few feet away. "Yes," he said softly, "I could see why that would make things difficult."

Ceara rested her hand on his forearm. "Don't be so sad, Daniel." A hint of that lovely smile returned. "She won't be your student forever. Ask me again in June, and I think you'll find my tune has changed." With that, she exited the car, retreating to her own.

Daniel watched her get settled behind her steering wheel, waving as she pulled out of her parking spot. A slow smile spread across his face. June was barely five months away.

He had a sense that this school year might end up feeling like the longest one yet. No matter. He could wait. For Ceara O'Connor, he could wait.

3

JUNE 10, 1 AE

Today, Harper and I were in the master bedroom in the farmhouse that's officially been claimed as our new home. Harper and I designated the master bedroom as the clinic, at least for now. To busy our minds from the weight of Sarah's and Ky's deaths, not to mention the absence of Biggs and the twins, we decided to move furniture around for a more efficient clinic. We also stocked the cabinets, shelves, and drawers with supplies Jake and Sanchez recently brought back from a scavenging trip. And when Harper asked me to steal some of the lollipops from the pantry downstairs to stash up here for Annie, I laughed because I'd already done it. While he thought it was amusing that we were on the same wavelength, I told him that it's because we're both awesome.

Harper is one of my best friends. He's like a brother to me, and it's weird to think that someone so important to me is not fully known by his closest friends and will one day be forgotten. In the future, when we're gone, people won't know of him. They won't know of any of us. They'll likely wonder about the first survivors and what became of them, but they won't think about us as real, knowable people. They won't know who we were or where we came from. One hundred years from now, we'll be an invisible stepping stone.

But Harper is special. Had he not enlisted in the military, I would never have met him. He would never have saved other survivors or delivered the first twins of the apocalypse. He embodies the best of who we are. There is a selflessness about him that no one in this life has had the honor of seeing but me.

Today, I saw a glimpse of his life before. I saw his mom, skin dark, green eyes gleaming under a raised, skeptical eyebrow as she looked at him. The corner of her mouth twitched with a smile—a tick of hers that he misses all the time. I felt his love for her and his sisters, and I understood his devotion to his father. I saw Harper when he was only Dustin, waggling eyebrows and all.

It's not my place to tell anyone else, but I'm writing it down for you, future Endingers, so that you might catch a small glimpse of how human we still are and where we came from. Where you came from, I suppose. Harper is one of the best men I know, and I can't imagine this world we're in without him.

Dustin sat in the lumpy chair beside his father's hospital bed, staring down at the sleeping, ashen-faced man beside him. Frank Harper, veteran, furniture salesman, lady charmer, loving father, and devoted husband, was dying. Cancer seemed to do that to most men in the family—throat, bone, lung—and in Frank's case it had started in the pancreas. Unlike the resentment that splintered the island, Hawaiians versus haoles, cancer didn't choose a side. Cancer didn't care how wonderful Frank was, how beloved. It was taking him away from his son, three daughters, and wife of twenty-seven years regardless of the sort of life he lived.

"Son," Frank rasped, peeling his eyes open. Dustin pried his gaze away from his father's soft, wrinkled hand and looked into his dulling gray eyes. "You take care of your mother and your sisters," he said, so raspy and slow Dustin could hear the rattle in his breath. "You are the man of the house now. You have to look after them for me."

Without hesitation, Dustin nodded and tried to swallow the anger and pain, the heartache. "I will, Dad." Dustin's young face was pinched, his nostrils flaring.

"You are a good boy," Frank said with a twitch of his lips. "My favorite son."

Dustin smiled, despite himself. "I'm your only son," he said, trying not to let his eyes fill with tears.

"That's why you're the best." With a slight incline of his head, Frank licked his lips and swallowed slowly, thickly, as though he had to force himself to. "You finish high school—you work hard. You take care of the girls, and I'm not talking about the ones at school." Frank tried to smirk, and a tear rolled down Dustin's cheek, though he quickly wiped it away. "It's okay to cry," Frank said, his own eyes shimmering. "I hoped to make it longer for you kids, but when it's your time—" He started to cough and Dustin jumped to his feet. "I'm alright," his father wheezed. "You should get your mother in here, though." *Before it's too late* went unsaid.

Dustin nodded, but he hesitated to let go of his father's hand as memories of the two of them—of the family, together—flooded his mind.

...The two of them working to build the front porch on week-days after school.

...The first time Dustin tried a sip of his father's beer—the face he made and the sound of his father's throaty laughter.

...The family at the beach on Sunday afternoons, Frank telling his daughters to put more clothes on, them telling him it was the beach and they were supposed to wear bathing suits.

...Dustin and his father at survival and emergency preparedness courses at the community college. "To take care of the girls should something devastating happen," Frank had claimed. Dustin was okay with that; he'd always wanted to be a war hero like his father. He'd always wanted to follow in his father's footsteps and make him proud.

But the happy memories faded as reality crashed over Dustin once more. He knew he would never have this man—his father—in his life again, and he let out a wail of heartbreak into his father's hand.

Dustin leaned against the front desk at Emilio's Gym, staring up at the latest news report on the television of a dozen more soldier casualties in the latest small-arms-fire battle with the Taliban. While his family was the most important thing in the world to him, especially since his father's death, there was still a small, not-so-silent part of him that yearned to follow in his father's footsteps. The desire to serve and protect his potential brothers-in-arms wasn't something that ever seemed to fade, and the mention of casualties on just about every news station made it even more difficult for Dustin to forget his longing to serve his country, even if it was both fear and duty that stirred in him.

"Hey, Dustin!" Tiffany called as she walked out of the bathroom with a bag of dirty towels. He yawned, already exhausted after working a few extra hours at the restaurant last night. Tiffany tossed the bag of dirties to Dustin—part of their daily routine since he was covering the desk for her—and he dropped them behind the counter. "You totally almost missed that," she said with a laugh.

"Yeah, well, I had a long night," he said, his eyebrows waggling.

Tiffany rolled her eyes. "I'm sure."

She was probably the only person who knew he was all flirt and no game. Not that he didn't actually have game, but he just didn't have the time to play it. Tiffany and Dustin had tried a relationship a few years back, when Dustin first started at the gym, but he was too busy most of the time to be very attentive to their relationship, especially with two jobs, three sisters, and a mother who would always come first. Tiffany understood. Harper knew she found his devotion to his family annoying sometimes but that she loved him all the more for it.

Tiffany nodded toward the machine room. "Now, get out of here," she said, stepping behind the counter. "Your five-o'clock is early—I saw her on the treadmill."

His brow crinkled as he shoved the last bite of his granola bar in his mouth. "How the hell did I miss that?"

She scrunched up her face. "Say it, don't spray it," she muttered. "You were probably digging around in your Mary Poppins bag of snacks when she walked in." She watched as Dustin zipped up his gym bag, eyeing a bag of cut carrots, blueberries, and trail mix. Tiffany gathered the class schedules strewn out on the countertop and began to organize them into a neat pile. "How can you eat so much—it's like all day, *every* day."

With another megawatt smile, he flexed his muscles. "If you want this," he said, lifting up his bag, "you eat this." He tossed his duffel into the employee room behind him. "It's a small price to pay for male perfection, am I right?" His eyebrows danced again, and Tiffany tried not to smile as she looked away.

"You're so ridiculous."

"We can't all be cute as a bug's ear, like you."

"Fantastic," Tiffany said, shaking her head. "That's just what every woman wants to hear." She speared Dustin with a pointed stare. "Now, get out of here. Shirley is waiting for you."

With a laugh, Dustin headed around the counter, swooping down to kiss Tiffany on the temple. "You're so cute," he said in a baby voice, trying to make her smile one last time.

She gaped at him. "And you're so inappropriate. I'm pretty sure that's sexual harassment in the workplace."

"You won't tell anyone," he called over his shoulder and stepped into the machine room. Dustin wondered when he'd gone from thinking Tiffany was cute in a roll-around-in-the-sheets way to a like-a-little-sister sort of way. And then he wondered if that's even what he felt at all.

He forgot his meandering thoughts the moment he spotted Shirley, his longest—and eldest—client. She was the one he adored the most, and he smiled as he stopped beside her treadmill.

"There you are," Shirley said the moment she spotted him.

Dustin grinned at her, wide and genuinely happy to see she was still her same old self, going at a snail's pace on the treadmill, exactly as he'd told her to. "Look at you go, girl," he said and glanced at her timer. She had five minutes left of her warm-up. "I think you've even broken a sweat and I haven't even started torturing you yet." He winked, and her smile widened, face flushing.

"Yes, well, you know how I feel about torture," she said, returning his wink.

With a throaty chuckle, Dustin shook his head. "You're killing me, Shirley." He loved their banter; it was the perfect way to end his day.

"What can I say? The only reason I even do my hair on Mondays is because I know I'll see you. I have to look my best."

"You always do." He nodded toward the weights. "I'll be over there when you're finished."

She shut her treadmill off and slowed to a stop. "I'm ready now. I want to get my money's worth." Shirley smirked and followed Dustin over to the weights.

He picked an unoccupied spot on the floor and pulled out a yoga mat for her, a newer one—not sticky, per her request. Dustin unrolled it onto the cement floor and nodded to it. "Alright now, show me what the past two years have done for you. I want stretches, you know the drill. Two sets, ten of each stretch. Then we'll move on to the heavy lifting."

Dustin picked up her half-empty water bottle. "I'll fill this up for you, but no cheating while I'm gone, now." He wagged a finger at her and headed off to the hydration station.

"Careful, Dustin," Tiffany said as she strode past him with a stack of clean towels in her arms. "Steph'll be jealous if she sees you flirting with Shirley."

"Good," he joked and stopped at the fountain. Dustin filled Shirley's bottle, watching her from the corner of his eye. "I don't hear you grunting," he called. "I hope you're not pooping out on me already, darlin'. I have a big day planned for you."

When Shirley groaned, he shook his head, laughing to himself and loving his job for all the fun he got to have, then headed back toward her. Despite his long hours at the gym and at his uncle's restaurant, it was his clients—the relationships he had with people—that kept him going and gave him something to look forward to when life started getting to him.

After forty-five minutes of stretches, some weight lifting, and a cooldown, Dustin said goodbye to his best girl. "See you next week, Shirley. Don't forget to tell Eddie I'm ready for him whenever he wants to get off that couch. A broken hip is no excuse," he teased and winked at Shirley one last time, pulling the door open for her. She threw her head back, laughed, and walked out the door.

When Dustin spotted Stephanie coming around the corner, he held the door open for her. She sauntered in after passing Shirley, and Dustin took a time-out to appraise her—long, dark brown hair, pulled up in a high ponytail that bounced each time she took a step, and her oh-so-tight yoga pants that hugged her curves perfectly. She met his gaze with a lifted eyebrow.

"Why do you encourage her?" Stephanie asked and looked back outside, watching Shirley drive away in her Cadillac.

"Encourage what?" Dustin released the door, letting it shut. "She's a flirt, and I flirt back."

Stephanie rolled her eyes, which elicited a smile from Dustin. "Someone's jealous of Shirley," he teased.

"Definitely not," Stephanie said as she walked behind the

counter. She opened the employee room door and headed back to her locker.

"Don't lie, Steph. You're regretting rejecting me at the Christmas party two years ago—it's eating away at you, admit it." He winked at Tiffany, who was looking on, mildly entertained by their daily banter.

"You know," Stephanie said, peeling off her long sleeves, "I think you say that every day because you want it to be true, but just because you keep saying it doesn't mean that it is."

Dustin shrugged and grabbed his water bottle from behind the counter. "Whatever you say. I'm hitting the treadmill, then the shower. If you decide you want to join…"

"Once again, inappropriate," Tiffany warned, but Dustin just laughed as he headed out toward the machines. He only had an hour before his late shift at the restaurant.

The next morning, just as the sun was rising over the North Pacific Ocean, Dustin came in from his morning run. He only had a few hours of sleep under his belt, though he tried not to think about that. He stretched outside his family's bungalow, one foot on the top step, the other outstretched behind him. It was mornings like this one, with a rich, indigo sea meeting the pale blue sky, that gave him pause when he considered life somewhere else. Well, it was the beauty of Hawaii *and* his family that gave him pause. Thoughts of a different life snuck into his mind more frequently these days, but Dustin continued to push them away. His family was here—work was here. What he had planned for his life had just shifted a little; it wasn't a big deal. The army could wait.

With a final stretch, Dustin walked to the front door and opened the screen door extra slowly so as not to wake anyone at the early morning hour.

When he stepped into the house, he spotted his mother standing at the stove in her robe, whisking a pan of eggs. "Mom, what are you doing up this early? You had a late shift last night."

"So did you," she said with a quick glance his way. She nodded to the pitcher of orange juice on the kitchen table. "Now, drink," she demanded. "And wash your hands and sit down to your breakfast."

Dustin walked over to his mother and kissed her temple. "You didn't have to get up to make me breakfast, Mom."

"Yes, I did. You work your butt off, you deserve a good breakfast, at least. Now go wash up, and get your sister."

"Jasmine?" he asked, clarifying which one, though he was sure he didn't need to.

His mother nodded. "The poor girl pulled another all-nighter," she clarified. "She has that biology exam this morning."

"That's right," Dustin said, drying off his hands. "She's been pretty stressed about it."

His mother handed him a glass of OJ. "She wouldn't be so stressed if she would give herself a break," she groused. "She wants you to be proud of her, you know?"

Dustin nodded, knowing full well that his sister was more than aware of how hard he and his mother had to work to put her and her sisters through school. Though he admired her for her hard work, he'd told her time and again that she didn't have to run herself into the ground on his account. *"You do it,"* was always her reply.

Dustin took a gulp of his juice, then headed down the hall toward Jasmine's bedroom. She would be sitting at her desk, probably half asleep from staying up all night because she refused to let them down. She wanted them to be proud of her.

Quietly, Dustin opened the door to keep from waking his middle sister, Victoria, who snored softly in the bed across the room.

Jasmine raised her head from her desk. Her bleached hair was stark against her dark islander skin. She flashed him a sleepy smile, bleary-eyed and rumpled from lack of sleep.

Dustin stepped inside, the faint scent of stale coffee tickling his nose. He wiped the accumulating sweat from his brow and leaned over her, looking down at her desk. Her neon flashcards were organized by color, and the writing on them was so small he could barely make out what they said. "That looks…frightening," he whispered and messed up her hair even more. "Come on, Mom made us early birds some breakfast."

Smoothing out her hair, Jasmine uncurled her legs from under her and rose to her feet and stretched. She whimpered as though she hadn't felt something so enlivening in years.

With a quiet laugh, Dustin ushered her out the door and eased it shut behind them. Victoria would appreciate being left to sleep in until it was time for her to get up for school.

"—coming tomorrow," his mother said quietly as Dustin stepped into the kitchen.

"Who's coming tomorrow?" he asked.

She didn't bother looking at him as she turned back to the stove. "Your uncle David is stopping by to look at my truck."

"Mom," Dustin said, pulling out the placemats and silverware to set the table. "I can do that shit for you. You don't need to call Uncle—"

"Language," she warned, pointing to his usual chair. "Your sister can set the table. Finish your juice."

Dustin flashed Jasmine a you-better-do-it look. She yawned again and pushed her chair out to rise to her feet.

"When are you meeting with that recruiting friend of yours again?" his mother asked, setting a plate of eggs and bacon on the table in front of him. "Rick—Richard, I think it was."

Dustin bit into a piece of bacon. "It's Ray, and he's not my friend. I haven't seen him at the gym in a while, which is fine. I have enough going on right now."

His mother stood beside him, silent, until he finally looked up at her. "At the rate you're going, you'll be dead before you have time to do much of anything, Dustin."

"I doubt that's true—"

"Jasmine," his mother said sharply, interrupting him. "When was the last time your brother had a day off?"

Jasmine shrugged. "I don't know. A while?"

"Uh-huh. And how many years now has he been planning to enlist in the Army?"

She snorted. "Uh—all his life," Jasmine said, easily enough.

"I see." His mother looked to him. "And yet here he sits."

"Ma, what do you want me to do? Leave you and the girls while I run off and—"

"Have an adventure?" she finished for him. "Live your own life?"

He looked from his mother to his sister and back, not appreciating them ganging up on him so early in the morning. "It's barely seven. Can we discuss this later?" It didn't matter what his mother said, he wasn't going to up and leave the four of them. His mother worked hard enough as it was to put the girls through college, and he didn't want his absence to be something else for her to worry about.

"Sure, but we *will* finish this conversation." She put a few pieces of extra-brown toast on his plate. "Eat your breakfast. You have to be off soon."

Ravenous and relieved to drop the topic for now, Dustin inhaled his breakfast. He didn't bother telling his mother that there was nothing else to discuss. As long as the girls had college tuitions and needed school supplies—as long as his mother had to work her fingers to the bone and bear the responsibility of being the sole parent for her children—he would never relent. She would just have to deal with that.

Between shifts at Emilio's and the restaurant, Dustin headed home for a quick bite and a change of clothes. The instant he turned the Jeep onto his street and spotted a red Camaro parked in front of his house at the end of the cul-de-sac, he knew something was up. Not only was it a car he'd never seen before, but it was nice and expensive with its blacked-out rims and tinted windows. A car like that was hard to miss.

Dustin pulled the Jeep to a stop behind the Camaro, leaving a space in the driveway for Jasmine to park when she got home from class. Eyeing the doorway suspiciously, he grabbed his gym bag, hauled his tired body out of the Jeep, and walked up the path to the bungalow's screen door. He could hear his mother's laugh—deep and throaty—over the sound of the waves crashing down the cliff behind the house. Then he heard the baritone chuckle of a man.

Dustin paused and swallowed in confusion, then opened the door to step into the house. The screen door creaked as it closed behind him, and he dropped his bag on the floor by the door.

A tall, unfamiliar Asian man dressed in Army fatigues was sitting at one end of the overstuffed couch in the living room, Dustin's mother perched on the edge of a cushion at the other end. The stranger smiled at Dustin, placing his hands on his knees to stand. "You must be Dustin," he said. He looked to be about thirty-five, ten or so years older than Dustin. A silver eagle badge adorned his BDU, and Dustin knew exactly who he was. Or rather *what* he was.

He looked at his mother. "A recruiter?"

"Indeed I am," the recruiter said, extending his hand. "It's nice to finally meet you in person, son. I've heard a lot about you. I'm Sergeant Konno."

"Sergeant," Dustin said, taking his hand. "I—it's nice to meet you. I'm sorry, but I'm just a little surprised. I wasn't expecting you." Dustin looked at his mother, who had a stalwart look on her face. A warning.

"Sergeant Konno has replaced your friend Ray," she explained.

"Ray-Ray shipped out a couple months ago," Sergeant Konno explained.

"Anyway," his mother said, "I'm glad you're home." She stood partway and leaned over the coffee table to pour Dustin a glass of iced tea. "Sit." She nodded to the recliner beside her spot on the couch, her tone brooking no argument, as usual.

So Dustin did the only thing he could. He sat down.

His mother handed him the glass, then raised her own to her lips, took a sip, and nodded to the Sergeant. "I asked Sergeant Konno to stop by and have a quick chat about—"

"Ma—"

"Don't interrupt me," she chided. "I invited Sergeant Konno to come over to talk to me about the enlistment process and what sort of commitment we're looking at when you finally do enlist. I wanted to learn more about it, since you won't tell me."

Dustin leaned back in the chair, rubbing his forehead.

"I don't mean to ruffle any feathers," the Sergeant said. "I ran into your mother at the diner, and she mentioned you'd been busy with work but that you were still interested in the Army. I told her I'd be happy to talk to you—both of you—if you had any questions."

"But I don't have questions," Dustin said, his tone a bit more clipped than he'd intended. "*She* is the one with questions, but you're just wasting your time here. I'm not leaving. It's not happening."

"Well, then you don't have to listen, but Sergeant Konno is going to tell *me* more about it—the signing bonus, the career opportunities…" She leaned back against the arm of the chair and nodded happily for the sergeant to continue.

At the mention of signing bonuses, Dustin's synapses started firing in a frenzy, and he wondered what the compensation might be for enlisting. Although he knew there was compensation for being in the military, he'd never really considered that it would be a viable alternative to him working several jobs here at home.

"As I was telling your mother before you arrived," Konno went on, "your compensation depends on the term of your contract. Obviously, the longer you sign up to serve the United States Army, the larger the signing bonus. And there is an array of career options as well. Where you'd be sent for basic training would depend on what your area of focus would be and where your aptitude tests place you."

Dustin didn't have time for this right now; he was exhausted, his mind spinning with the rising tide of questions. He felt more than a little frazzled. "Mother"—he stood up—"can I speak with you outside, please?" He gave the door a pointed look.

His mother nodded graciously and smiled at the recruiter. "Give us just a moment, please."

Dustin crossed the room and stepped out onto the porch he'd built with his father nine years ago, waiting for his mother to join him. It was strange how much had changed since his father's death, yet how much felt the same.

His mother gently shut the screen door and followed Dustin down the steps, away from the house.

"Ma—"

"Listen to me," she said softly. "This is not your life." She took his hands in hers. "You are doing this because you are a wonderful man, just like your father, but you are not happy, not really."

"Yes, Ma, I am happy."

"No, you are content because you are doing what you feel is right, but it isn't necessary. You are allowed to live the life you wanted. Your father would agree. You've put in your time with us, Dustin. You've sacrificed enough. It's not right for your sisters to get whatever they want while you sacrifice everything for them. You're their brother, not their father. You deserve to have a life of your own." She gave his hands a squeeze. "You haven't even been out with a girl in months—"

"I hardly think that's important right now."

"Don't sass me; it is important. You are only twenty-four, you shouldn't be this exhausted already. Your father would want you to be just as happy as the rest of us."

"Maybe, but he would want me to do everything I can to—"

"Dustin Anthony Harper, who do you think knew him better, you or me?"

Dustin's patience thinned. "I knew him well enough."

His mother reached up and cupped his cheek with her hand. "He's gone from us, sweetheart. I have three perfectly capable daughters who are spoiled rotten by their big brother and could use a job a handful of hours a week—you've done enough for now. We will miss you, of course, and it will take a while to get used to you being gone, but we will be fine without you. I promise you that."

Dustin thought of Victoria, who would be eighteen next year, and he knew he'd only ever have to worry about her getting so sucked into the television that she might forget to eat something. He thought of Charlotte and how she would be starting high school next year, and how she'd likely be a handful, but that Jasmine would help his mother whip her into shape. Then he thought of his iron-willed mother, who loved them unconditionally and had the strength to keep their lives running like a well-oiled machine.

"I know you would be fine," he admitted, though the thought of leaving them sent a wave of sadness crashing over him.

"Which is why I am not worried in the slightest," she said. "Besides, we're not in this alone. We have friends and family that love us and will help us." She eyed Dustin for a moment. "You want to do what you believe your father would've expected of you, but I am the one who is alive, Dustin. I see you every day, and I know you're not happy, not truly. No matter what you say."

Dustin's heart tightened at the thought of his father, at remembering his death and the bleakness that followed. "Things are finally starting to feel a little normal again," he said. Though it had been nine years, the first couple had been spent in mourning, the next few in rebuilding their lives.

"Which means it's time for you to start a new chapter."

An old Honda Accord with muffled, bass-thumping music pulled up in front of the house, coming to a stop behind Sergeant Konno's Camaro. Victoria hopped out of the passenger seat, sticking her head back into the car to exchange a few words with her friend before shutting the car door, taking a step back, and waving goodbye. She turned and headed toward the house.

"Vic," Dustin's mother called, not taking her eyes off of her son.

"Yeah?" Victoria stopped on the middle stepping stones that led to the house, her dark hair pulled up in a bun atop her head.

"What do you think of your brother going into the Army?"

Victoria shrugged, then continued on toward the house. "It's about time. Bring back some hot friends," she said, the screen door slamming shut behind her.

His mother laughed. "See?"

Though his chest tightened with fear and uncertainty and possibility, Dustin couldn't help but laugh. "Alright," he said. "I'll think about it."

4

DECEMBER 16, 1 AE

I met my mom today for the first time in person—the infamous Dr. Anna Wesley of Peterson Airforce Base, bringer of death and mastermind behind the Virus that killed off almost everyone and mutated everyone else. She'd saved me from Clara on the golf course, but I hadn't been me and I didn't know who she was, not really, so that doesn't count.

I met Peter, too. To think that only months ago I thought my mom was dead is a major head trip. I have a mom. I have a half-brother. And, on top of that, Jason and I are what started this entire apocalypse, with my mom and dad in the very center of it. It's still somewhat unbelievable, even after knowing so much. The General, what he's done and what he did to my family all those years ago—it's all so much clearer now that I see it unfolding in my mind like a horror film I can't tear my gaze from.

And today, after flying in from Central California, where Carl and Randall were keeping me as their personal blood bank, I rode in a wagon with my mom and Peter. I saw things—so many things—memories, fears, hopes…things too big to ignore. I saw how it all started, or at least all of the important bits.

My mom could've nulled me—after all, Jason gets his Ability from somewhere—but she didn't. She wanted me to see—to know—everything. It was sort of a silent gift she was giving me, a way of paying a debt, I think. And, after all of these years of not knowing or understanding, it was the most heartbreaking, honest, and real gift she ever could've given me.

In a little hidden cove south of Bodega Bay, Anna sat on the beach on a bright blue blanket, content and humming as she bounced her one-year-old daughter on her lap.

"Hear the birdies?" she asked softly, her eyes opened wide, mimicking Zoe's as she watched, astonished by the gulls drifting and calling high above.

It was Anna's favorite time of year—the days finally growing longer, with fuchsia and yellows and greens hugging the jagged, seaside cliffs that stretched in either direction. She was in her own hidden haven, a mother having a Sunday afternoon outing with her two beautiful children and her wonderful husband. For a family with too many secrets, it was a relief to go unnoticed…to just blend in. Tom's ability to alter the perception of others and Anna's ability to amplify his efforts stopped people from asking too many questions. They were such a great team. It often brought a smile to Anna's face when she considered how well they'd pulled it off. They'd escaped. She was free and happy. *They* were happy.

"You better hurry!" Tom chuckled, and Anna watched Jason squeal and shriek as he ran on suntanned legs away from the encroaching waves. "Come on, run faster," Tom urged, his chuckle deepening when Jason stumbled in the wet sand.

Anna's family was her life now; that's what she had to remember. The days when she'd first left Colorado and feared that she would never be able to break the tethers to her past were all a foggy, nightmarish memory.

Gurgles and elongated vowel sounds brought Anna's attention

back to Zoe, who was blissfully occupied on her lap. The moment her daughter's clear blue eyes shifted to hers and Zoe's chubby cheeks rounded with a smile, Anna felt a twinge of selfish satisfaction. No matter the repercussion of her past actions, she wouldn't have changed a single decision if doing so meant her children would never have been born and this perfect day on the beach would never have happened. This moment of pure happiness was worth it.

Anna brushed Zoe's soft, alabaster cheek with the back of her index finger. She excelled in the lab, but motherhood was what she'd been meant for; this family, *these* children, felt more right than anything ever had before.

Leaning forward, Zoe clawed at the sand, awed as it poured through her stubby fingers. Anna had to stop her from bringing the next handful up to her mouth. "Don't eat that, sweetie, it's icky," she said, laughing softly. She reveled in her daughter's curiosity, her constant movement and the way her eyes animated with mischief. Zoe would be like her in many ways, Anna knew. She just hoped she'd only passed on the better parts of herself to her little girl.

Despite the blazing sun, Anna shivered.

With an "Oooh," Zoe stared down at her hand and then at the sea of sand.

"Feels nice, huh, Zo?" Anna smiled, watching as deep contemplation scrunched her daughter's features.

Another bark of laughter brought their attention back up to Tom. "Look out, Son," he said as he reached for Jason's hand, helping to hold him up against the crashing waves. But, stubborn as he was, Jason pulled away from his father and succumbed to the tumbling water that swirled around his little body.

With chattering teeth, Jason struggled to his feet. His shoulders were pink from the sun and sand clung to his knees, but he was determined. He was on his feet and running out into the roiling blue water again even as it prepared for its next assault.

"Sometimes I wonder if he'll ever grow tired of this game," Tom said, voice raised to reach Anna's ears. He flashed her the same heart-stopping smile that had brought her out of darkness many times before their escape and turned back to Jason.

Anna admired her husband as he ran his fingers through his damp, brown hair. He'd grown a little grayer over the past decade, but he was handsome and kind and strong, just as he'd always been. He had practically moved mountains for her, had saved her in so many ways and allowed her this gift of a family, of happiness. Not a day went by that she didn't appreciate that.

Once again, Anna tried not to think about how different things would've been had she stayed in Colorado. She'd been so afraid to leave she almost shrugged off Tom's offer to whisk her away and start a better life together. Her chest grew heavy under the immensity of her decision to leave her work behind. Her life would have been so different, so empty, had she said no to him.

"Honey, you okay?" Tom's voice stirred Anna from those unwanted thoughts as he approached.

When she saw his broad smile and felt his warm, pale blue eyes on her, she smiled back. She nodded in response, drinking in the sight of him. Thanks to him, she was okay. He had a calming effect on her, something so natural it happened without her realizing it most of the time.

When Jason shouted in laughter, Anna's gaze quickly skirted over to him. He was squealing, running toward them on the dry beach. "We should go soon," she said. "I think he's had enough sun for today."

Jason's groan carried on the breeze as he jogged up. "But Mom…"

Grinning despite himself, Tom said, "No whining, Son. If your mom says it's time to go, we'd better not argue with her. She cooks our dinner, after all."

Jason plopped down beside her, sand spraying all around him.

"Be careful around your sister, please," Anna said, all patience and motherly concern as she brushed away the wet sand peppering Zoe's lap. She tilted her head and beamed inwardly as she watched Jason gently brush a few stray granules from his sister's chubby, white leg.

"But you said we could be here all day." Although his voice was low and quiet, it wasn't quite a whine.

Holding in a grin, Anna gave her son a warning look. "I said for the *afternoon*. It's been four hours, sweetheart. You're so cold your teeth are going to rattle right out of your little head." She rumpled his damp hair before gathering up a couple of Zoe's toys and dropping them into her floral-print beach bag. "Plus, it's almost time for dinner. Do you still want to help me make pizzas?"

"Yeah!" The excitement in Jason's eyes told her his disappointment about leaving had already faded away.

Anna reached into the beach bag and tossed her shivering son a towel. "Dry off, then help me with your sister, please."

And, like they'd done almost every weekend over the summer months, Anna, Tom, and Jason gathered up their things, the sound of the Pacific breaking against the cliffs their only farewell.

"Here," Tom said, flinging his damp towel over his shoulder. He reached down for Zoe, allowing Anna the free hands she needed to brush off her favorite white eyelet skirt and adjust her floppy, oversized hat.

"Thank you," she breathed, collecting their garbage and lunch leftovers and stowing everything in her bag. "So," she started nonchalantly, "when did you get that gash on your palm?" She lifted an eyebrow and peered up at him. "I don't recall it being there last night."

Tom lifted a shoulder, pretending indifference.

With an audible sigh, Anna shook her head. "I thought you were taking Sundays off. I'm sure the Petersons wouldn't want you spending your only day off working on their barstools." Although she wasn't surprised he'd been out in his woodshop in the wee hours of the morning, she couldn't help but give him crap for it.

"It was only for an hour or so," he lied and, with a smirk, held out his pinky for Zoe to grab ahold of. He always lost himself in his work, sketching a schematic or sanding a knot in a piece of wood to utter perfection. An hour to him meant three cups of cold coffee and a missed meal. Although this was something Anna knew would never change, it often resulted in a scornful scowl on her face all the same. "Besides," he said, "you're always telling Jason that every scar reminds us of how strong we are, so I must be pretty strong." He winked and flashed her his pearly whites.

She made a noncommittal noise. "You're hilarious, Tom. Simply hilarious."

"I'm ready," Jason sang. He handed his mom his wet towel. "Pizza! Pizza! Pizza!" he said, jumping up and down in excitement.

"Are you going to help Mommy cook dinner too?" Tom asked little Zoe, bouncing her in his arms. Zoe reached for his nose in answer.

"No, Zoe's not going to help Mommy with dinner," Anna replied with an unamused laugh. "*Daddy*'s going to play with her while Mommy gets big brother cleaned up and dinner ready." She rose on tiptoes and planted a firm kiss on Tom's lips. "And Mommy's going to have a glass of merlot while she does it."

"Diving right into the good stuff, I see," he teased with a smirk.

Anna nodded. "You bet." She shook off the blue blanket before she folded it quickly and shoved it into the already-full bag, then gathered an anxious Zoe back into her arms. "Jason, sweetheart," Anna called to him. He was headed toward the pathway up the hill, reciting his favorite television song as he dragged his feet in the sand. "Don't forget your sea glass!" Anna pointed to the collection of smoothed green and white glass that he'd piled next to the giant boulder he sometimes turned into a fort.

"Oh, yeah!" Jason jogged over to his treasure, setting each piece of glass carefully into his palm to make sure he didn't drop a single one. Though they weren't sharp, he knew glass was dangerous, and he took every precaution as he counted each and every piece for his collection at home.

Finally, with Tom's arm around her shoulders, Zoe cooing in her arms, and Jason running and spinning as he made his way up the trail ahead of them, Anna headed for home.

The next day, after giving Zoe a bath, washing and folding two loads of laundry, and attempting to plant the rest of her gladiola bulbs on the west-facing side of the house, Anna glanced up at the clock and realized she was running late.

"Shit," she breathed and bent down to pick up Zoe from her playpen in the center of the living room. "You didn't hear Mommy say that, sweetheart. 'Shit' is a bad word."

Zoe simply peered at her with questioning eyes as she reached out to touch the onyx hair hanging around Anna's face. "We've got to pick up your brother from school, and we're going to be late." She hadn't even gotten to work on the magazine article she'd planned to finish before the deadline. Best-laid plans of a stay-at-home mom.

Quickly, Anna took Zoe upstairs. She proceeded to change out of her ratty housework clothes into a linen skirt and red tank top. She ran a brush through her hair, then collected Zoe's baby bag before rushing out the front door. The Little Critters Playhouse, the local preschool, wasn't very far away—about a mile or so—but Anna knew she'd have twenty-plus mothers to contend with when it came to parking in the tiny cul-de-sac where it was located.

Once she had Zoe strapped into her baby seat, Anna sat in the driver's seat of the Wagoneer and hauled the door closed. With a turn of the key, the engine roared to life and she backed out of the driveway.

On the drive to Little Critters, Anna wondered if she'd ever find the time to finish the article she'd promised the *American*

Scientist Journal by the end of the month. She only had a couple weeks left, and she was cutting it close. Genetic biomarkers were her specialty, or at least the specialty of Dr. LouAnn Presley, her nonexistent alter ego. And what better way for a nondescript house mom to explore her scientific passions than through Dr. Presley's research of infectious diseases and their genetic effects on the body?

Anna slowed the car as she turned into the Montessori school's cul-de-sac. Children and parents were milling around outside the old sun-bleached school. As Anna pulled up behind a station wagon a dozen yards down the street, she groaned. The sidewalk and street were teeming with mothers holding hands with their children and children trying to keep up with their mothers' hurried footsteps as they clutched the day's artwork against their chests.

Anna climbed out of the Wagoneer and opened the backseat door, gathering Zoe into her arms. "Here we go, Zo," she muttered. "Time to step into the snake pit."

Anna didn't like navigating large groups. In spite of Tom's efforts to keep people's curiosity away from the Cartwright family, he couldn't stop the idle chatter of the bored, stay-at-home mothers who thought Anna and Tom were too private. Mothers always wanted to know things, to book playdates, or to invite the family over for dinner. While Anna was a practiced liar, she didn't enjoy doing it and preferred to avoid most conversations at all costs. Especially when it came to their overly concerned and newly single neighbor, Charlene Brent, who was currently walking straight toward her.

"Oh, Anna, you're here!" Charlene's shrill voice echoed over the chatter of the other mothers carrying on conversations with their children as they filed out of the building.

Anna plastered a perfected false smile on her face and lifted her gaze to greet Charlene. "Oh, hi!"

"I'm surprised to see you," Charlene said, her red-haired, squinty-faced, six-year-old daughter, Natalie, trudging along behind her. The poor child looked miserable and winced every time her mother spoke to her. Anna wished she could put her dislike of Charlene aside long enough to invite her over so little Natalie could play with Jason. But Anna didn't trust that smiley, eyelash-batting divorcée around her husband.

"Why wouldn't I be here?" Anna asked, all smiles and pleasantness.

"Oh, it's just that I figured you'd sent that nice gentleman standing over there with Jason to pick him up. Is he a family friend? Tom's brother, perhaps?" Her lips spread into a smile that Anna barely registered as her heartbeat skipped and she searched the crowd for Jason. "Not that I would know, given how private y'all are."

When Anna saw Jason walk up to the curb and gaze around, Anna excused herself and hurried toward him.

Jason smiled and waved as he stepped off the curb to meet her. Although it was a dead end and there was no traffic to speak of, he knew well enough to look both ways before he stepped onto any street. Anna looked around, wondering who the man Charlene had mentioned might've been, but saw no one unfamiliar. Seeing that Jason was okay, Anna pushed her worries aside and peered down at him, unsurprised to see that he was holding his Captain America comic.

Anna shook her head. "Oh, Tom," she muttered, then her smile brightened. "Hi, sweetheart. How was your day?" She moved Zoe from her right hip to her left and reached her hand out so Jason could take hold of it.

Jason shrugged. "It was okay."

"Yeah? Were you good for Miss Silver?" Anna asked, distracted. She scanned the thinning group of parents around her one last time. "Charlene said you were talking to a man a minute ago."

"Yeah," he said, unconcerned.

"Who was he? One of your friends' dads?" Anna ran her fingers through Jason's hair as they headed back to the car.

Jason shrugged again. "Some guy."

"A stranger? I thought we don't talk to strangers, J."

"He's not a stranger," he said. "He's your friend."

"*My* friend?" Anna tried to figure out who'd stopped by to say hi, though she could think of no one, especially not anyone Charlene didn't already know. Again, a sense of unease washed over Anna.

They made it back to the car, and Jason climbed into the back seat, buckling himself in next to Zoe. After Anna strapped Zoe back into her car seat, she paused. The hair on the back of her neck and down the backs of her arms stood on end. She turned around, but there was no one there.

After one last scouring glance, Anna turned back to shut the car door before she settled into the driver's seat.

"This secret friend of mine didn't tell you his name, sweetheart?" she asked, keeping her voice in check despite her racing heart. She peered back at Jason in the rearview mirror.

"No," he said, staring down at his opened comic book. "But he likes my Captain America comic." Jason grinned with pride.

Anna thought that was a strange thing to say. "Really? Why do you say that?"

"He's a soldier."

Anna's heart skipped a beat, and she felt her face heat and her body begin to shake as she turned in her seat to face her son. "How do you know that, sweetie?"

"He told me." Jason flipped quickly through the pages, pointing to the words in the quote bubbles like he was trying to read them.

With a painfully dry swallow, Anna faced forward, her mind overflowing with fear. A soldier? That meant one of two things—the very man they'd been hiding from had found them, or someone else had on his behalf. Either one was a terrifying prospect.

Anna jolted upright in bed, her body screaming that something wasn't right. "Tom," she rasped, running her fingers through her sweat-dampened hair. When her eyes focused in the darkness, she froze.

A shadowed figure sat at the foot of her bed.

Anna covered her mouth with her hands to stifle a shriek.

"You seem surprised to see me, my dear."

Anna's mind spiraled, her whole body trembling. He was here. In her house. He'd finally found her. The many ways her family was in real, grave danger tallied in her mind. Anna screeched, remembering her daughter's cradle beside her bed, and scrambled over to it, relieved to find Zoe still inside, asleep. Although Anna knew Gregory might try to hurt her children, he hadn't, not yet, and she tried to remain calm and think strategically despite the paralyzing fear creeping in. I know him—I know how Gregory thinks, *she reminded herself. And she knew what he wanted from her, too.*

Like flipping a switch corroded by time, Anna—hysterical wife and devoted mother—began to fade away, and Dr. Anna Wesley reemerged, cool, confident, and composed.

Though she'd known this day might come, she'd prayed it never would, and, stupidly, she'd allowed herself to forget to live in fear. She hadn't been prepared to find Gregory—her one true mistake and regret, the reason she'd left her old life behind—sitting at the foot of her bed, shrouded in shadows. Menace exuded from him.

"Gregory," she breathed, body shaking.

"Anna." He nodded to her, his certainty and power evident in the weight of her name on his tongue. "Surprised I found you and Miller, I see. I'm not sure why." He let out a small, bone-chilling laugh. "It was only a matter of time. More time than I would've

preferred, but then finding you in another man's bed isn't preferable either."

His voice was more detached than she recalled, more sinister, and his Ability was stronger. She could tell by his calmness, the threat in his tone. Given the time they'd been apart, Anna knew Gregory must've been provided plenty of opportunities to hone his mind-manipulation capabilities. Anna shuddered to think of how many innocent people he must have killed in order to find her, and she wondered why he wasn't attempting to use his Ability on her now. Not that it would do him any good, but he didn't know that.

"You were at my son's school today." Understanding cemented her worst fears. "You've been toying with me." Gregory knew about her children; he'd been watching them, interacting with them. Knowing this, Anna clung to the only thing she knew was true: she needed Gregory to stay out of her mind. She needed to stay clearheaded if she would have any chance of saving her family.

Eyes fixed on him, Anna gripped Tom's arm as hard as she could, her fingernails biting into his skin as she desperately and soundlessly tried to wake him.

"It's no use," Gregory said on an exhale. He rubbed his jaw like he might be disappointed. "He won't wake up."

Anna's nostrils flared, and the center of her chest felt like it was caving in. Stay calm, *she reminded herself.* Focus.

Anna swallowed and tried to keep her chin from trembling, blinking away the tears welling in her eyes. "What do you want from me, Gregory?"

Gregory glanced at the doorway.

That was all it took for another lick of fear to burn the backs of Anna's eyes, tears springing back into place. "Jason!" she screamed. The surmounting terror made her unsteady as she scrambled from the bed, her limbs heavy and awkward in her haste.

"You were mistaken if you thought I was going to make this

easy for you," he called from behind, but Anna was too petrified, running down the hall toward Jason's room. What was left of her strength dissolved, and she stood immobilized in Jason's doorway. An ear-piercing scream escaped from her throat.

His bed was empty, and a spattering of blood stained his sheets.

"Your children are gone, my dear. Forever, if you don't pay attention." His voice was carefully controlled, holding only a hint of annoyance. "You might as well sit down and listen to what I have to say."

But Anna heard none of his words. Rage and grief and fear completely consumed her. She ran at him, a mother's desperation driving her resolve and hatred. "You son of a bitch!" she shouted, her hand raised to strike him.

Gregory shot up from the edge of the bed and grabbed her wrist, a wicked smile on his face. "So you do still have some spark in you, I see. I was wondering." He pulled her closer, his fingers digging into her flesh in warning. "Now," he ground out, "you're going to listen to me, Anna darling, and you're going to do what I say, or your kids are dead."

If he killed them, then Gregory would have nothing to bargain with; there would be nothing left to force her hand. Gregory knew that. Anna had to believe Jason and Zoe really were still alive. "Where are my children? Take me to them, Gregory, and I'll do whatever you want. I swear it."

Clicking his tongue, Gregory shook his head. "Sorry, but that isn't how this works." He pulled her closer to him, wrapping his right arm around her waist. There was a lascivious, possessive gleam in his eyes that made Anna's stomach churn. Gregory's villainy was something she could never forget, and it made him predictable. But she'd forgotten how delusional he was, how sick. "You thought you could leave me, that I would just let you go?" he spat at her. "You're mine, darling, *and it seems that while you've been off playing house with Sergeant Miller, you've forgotten that one* very *important thing." He crushed his lips against hers with bruising pressure.*

Anna struggled against the strength of his hold, but his grip around her waist only tightened. He bit her lip, bringing tears of pain and disgust to her eyes. When Gregory finally pulled away, his eyes were filled with a lust more intense than anything Anna had ever seen before.

Anna shuddered, cringing away from him.

"I want you to come home with me, where you belong," he breathed, making her skin crawl even more. His cold, gray eyes scoured her face. "I know Miller has used his Ability to persuade you otherwise, but you belong with me, and as soon as I get you home, you'll remember that."

It wasn't obsession, desperation, or coercion that seethed from his words, but something more sinister and alarming. Whatever Gregory had planned for her, it wasn't something she was likely to survive unscathed.

"Bring me my family, Gregory, or I swear to God, I will—"

Gregory slapped her across the face. "You'll what? The day you left, you nearly ruined me," he hissed. "My plans shattered that night." His hand was on her throat, gripping her so tightly that Anna had to gasp for air. "Do you have any idea how much time and heartache you've caused me?" He watched her as she clawed at his grasp. "Lucky for you, I believe in second chances. I'm so close to my goals I can taste them, and you're going to help me take the final steps."

After another gut-wrenching kiss, Gregory let go.

Anna woke with a scream. She was drenched in sweat, and her heart hammered in her chest, each beat echoing in her ears as she gasped for air. Clamping her hand over her mouth, she stifled her unbidden sobs. She scoured the darkened room with tear-filled eyes, but she saw no one in the moonlight.

Frantically, Anna turned, relieved to find Zoe sleeping in the cradle beside the bed.

"Honey, are you alright?" She could hear Tom, hear the concern in his voice, but she was too panicked to think of anything other than the danger Jason was in. Anna crawled out from under the covers and stumbled on shaking limbs down the hallway to his room. She prayed he was still there, asleep.

He was.

Anna let out a strangled cry of relief. She rushed into the room and crouched beside his bed, scanning his sheets and clothes for blood, but found nothing. Her vision was blurred, but she sat on the floor, staring at her little boy, worried that if she blinked, if she closed her eyes for even a millisecond, he would disappear.

She wasn't sure how much time passed before she felt certain he would be okay, at least for now. She kissed the side of his cheek, causing him to stir from sleep a bit, but she didn't care that she'd disturbed him. Her heart filled with relief at the scent of his warm skin, the laundry detergent clinging to his pajamas, and the apple shampoo from his bedtime bath. Each rise of his chest was a reassurance that he was alright. That he was still alive. It had only been a nightmare. A terrible, gut-wrenching nightmare.

Hearing movement in the hallway, Anna looked to the doorway to find Tom standing there, watching her. His concern was palpable, and all Anna wanted was for him to hold her in his arms and promise her that Gregory would never *ever* find them. Though she feared it was too late for that. If her suspicions were right about the man at the school earlier that day, he'd already found them.

Her feet were moving before she realized it, and she went to Tom, trying to hold in the hysteria amplifying inside her.

"Shhh..." Tom pulled her to his chest and wrapped his arms around her, his embrace as protective as ever. Except now that sense of protection felt false. "It was only a dream," he told her.

Anna latched onto him, her nightmare all too fresh in her mind. "He was here, Tom, in our home," she rasped. "He killed you and

—and took the children…" She cried into his shoulder as he led her back to their bedroom and closed the door behind them. "It *wasn't* just a dream. I'm telling you, he's found us, Tom. I'm almost positive he was at Jason's school today, and now he's found a way into my dreams." She took a shuddering breath. "He's taunting me."

Tom paused at the foot of their bed and held Anna away from him by her shoulders as he searched her face. "Even if Gregory really is messing with your mind, that's all he's doing. He's just a man, Anna. You have to remember that."

"He's a monster," she said. "One that I created." The normal life they'd fashioned had never felt more like a lie.

"We've gotten away from him before," Tom whispered, pulling her against him once more. "We can do it again. Just calm down."

Anna shook her head.

"He can't touch us—you can null his Ability, and I can make us disappear again. We can leave right now and—"

"And go where?" she practically shouted. Her gaze flicked to Zoe to ensure she still slept in her cradle by the bed. Lowering her voice, she said, "Where can we possibly go that he can't find us? You've hidden us this long and he still found us, even with me amplifying your Ability." She peered up at him. "We can't win against him, Tom. He's grown too strong…he's controlling too many people…"

Tom stared down at her, sadness and concern softening his features.

"Don't you dare look at me like that," she snapped. "You know how horrible he is. How can you be so calm?"

Tom brushed a tear from her cheek. "I hate seeing you like this," he said, like he hadn't even heard her.

Anna covered her face and began to cry. This was all her fault. "What have I done?"

"Shhh," Tom soothed, holding her tight against him. "We'll figure this out. He's not going to attack us or take our children in the middle of the night. You know he's too smart for that. They're safe for now. You need to calm down so we can think."

Anna shook her head, unable to ignore the fear still seeping into her like water into parched, neglected earth. The sound of Gregory's voice was still so crisp and clear in her head. How had he gotten into her mind? The memory of blood on Jason's sheets brought more tears to her eyes.

Despite her husband's reassurances, Anna couldn't shake the dread that eroded the false sense of normalcy she'd too willingly adopted over the past ten years. Her past—all but forgotten—sprouted from the roots buried deep inside her.

Tom shushed her and rubbed her back in a slow, circular motion. The sound of his voice helped bring her back to the present. How could she possibly have forgotten how serious this was? How could she so easily have let her guard down? She'd been living a lie, a dangerous, potentially devastating lie.

Anna stepped out of Tom's embrace, taking a deep breath as she berated herself. "How did I let it get this far?" She peered around the room at the fabrication that had become her life. "How did I forget everything we went through…everything I did? If he releases the Virus…" She shook her head. "Our children will have no future. None at all. How did I ever think we could have a normal life?" When she registered Tom's silence, she looked at him.

Pensive, he stood at the foot of the bed, uncertainty furrowing his brow.

"What is it?" she asked. She knew that look. He was about to tell her something she wouldn't like. "What?" She closed the distance between them. "Tell me."

Tom let out a heavy exhale and held her gaze as some heavy emotion illuminated his eyes. "I made you forget," she barely heard him say.

Anna straightened. "You did *what*?" Her jaw clenched, ire masking her distress. She knew that altering her memories was all too possible a task for him. "What exactly did you make me forget, Tom?"

He reached for her, but Anna slapped his hand away and moved further away from him. "Tell me," she demanded.

"Anna, I had to—"

"No," she said, raising a hand. She was beginning to understand. She took an unsteady step backward. "You stole my memories? My fear?" Her eyes narrowed like she was searching his very soul for the missing parts of herself. "How could you do that to me?" Her voice was no longer weak and fragile, but brittle and fierce. "I'm your *wife*. How dare you even consider messing with my head."

Sitting down on the edge of the bed, Tom stared past her at a memory she couldn't see and let out another deep breath. "It was right after you lost the first baby," he explained, making Anna's heart plummet as she remembered the day she found out she'd miscarried. Not very delicately, the doctor had explained that he'd warned her about her stress level and constant state of overexertion being bad for the pregnancy. "You were so worried about finalizing the neutralizer, about him finding us—"

"A rightful fear, Tom!" She threw her hands in the air, deflecting the grief and guilt that suddenly resurfaced. She turned away from him. Her life felt tainted all over again, and she felt strangely alone. She couldn't even trust her own husband.

"I wouldn't have done it unless I had to, Anna. You know me better than that."

"I have no idea what I know anymore, thanks to you," she growled.

His pained expression hardened, and he stood and stepped toward her. His eyes gleamed accusingly in the evening light. "It was consuming you."

It killed our baby was left unsaid, but it hung in the gaping void between them.

Anna wiped the veil of tears from her eyes and jutted out her jaw to stay her quivering chin. Tom's gaze was too intense, and guilt screamed within her once more. She looked down at her bare feet and tried to stuff the resurfacing sense of loss and despair back down, to hide it somewhere deep within her.

"Anna," Tom whispered, running his hand down her bare arm. "Your fear of that man was taking you over—it was taking *us* over. I promised to protect you, in sickness and health, even if that means protecting you from yourself." He let the words sink in for a moment before he continued. "I wouldn't have done it if I hadn't felt it was necessary. Leaving Colorado was a decision *we* made. Having a family was *our* choice. We couldn't live every waking moment in fear. *I* couldn't do that, otherwise what the hell was it all for?" Anna met his gaze, and he searched her face as if looking for an ounce of understanding. "I love you, and I wasn't going to let *him* ruin us…ruin you. And no matter how angry you are with me, I know you at least see the sense in that."

Reluctantly, Anna nodded. She'd remembered the constant state of fear; her nightmare had ensured as much. She could feel it now, coursing through her, alive and clawing for control. It was a necessary reminder of what sort of life they lived now—and what they'd left behind—and how careful they needed to be, no matter how reckless they'd been over the years. She couldn't allow Tom to alter her memories again—her perception of fear. She couldn't afford to lose the justified paranoia in which they should be living each and every day.

Tom coaxed her back into his arms, and she went to him with silent tears streaming down her cheeks. She was angry, yes, but Tom had given her nearly a decade of reprieve that she would never have had otherwise. That she knew she'd never get again. Even though she appreciated his gift, she wasn't sure she could ever forgive him for it.

But she needed to worry about the future. Gregory had already made his first move. She had to be ready for his next.

Later that night, Anna stirred in bed. She'd been restless all night, unable to stop imagining all of the ways Gregory might come after her, or worse, her family. She pictured him manipulating Jason's mind, convincing him to hurt himself or his sister or forcing Jason to leave with him by making him think that he wanted to. Gregory no doubt knew doing so would kill her inside. He wasn't an impulsive man, which made him all the more frightening. He'd had years to come up with a well-thought-out plan, and that was what troubled her the most.

She could send the children to live with someone; she could hide them. But who did she know? Who did she trust? No one. She and Tom had gone to great lengths to keep to themselves. There was no one in Bodega Bay—or anywhere else in the world, for that matter—who she trusted enough to take in her children for who knew how long. She and Tom were the only people who could protect Jason and Zoe, the only people who knew just how special they were—how different. Nobody else could take care of them, so entertaining the idea was pointless.

Anna sighed and squeezed her eyes shut. She knew she would never sleep soundly again, not until she found a remedy to all of this. Not while Gregory was out there, probably watching them, toying with her and waiting to make his next move. There was only one other thing she could do besides wait helplessly for him to make his next move.

With that realization, she crawled out of bed, deciding it was time to dig up all of her old research papers and get back to work. The neutralizer was the only thing that gave her hope—it was her miracle. If she could complete the formula—if she could even get it *close* to perfection—she would head to Mare Island's pharmaceutical labs to test the serum. She could make whatever final adjustments were necessary there, then administer it to her family. She just needed Gregory's taunting to last a few more days.

Anna walked down the hall to Jason's room. Anxiety, suffocating and ever-present since she'd awoken from the nightmare, lifted a little when she saw her son sprawled out on his bed, sound asleep. His head was partially covered with his robot-patterned pillow. She crept into his room and pulled up the blanket wadded at Jason's feet. With a sigh, she ran her fingers through his dark hair before leaning in to kiss the side of his face. "I love you, my sweet boy," she whispered, then crept farther down the hall to her office.

All she could think about now was the work she had started—had abandoned—years ago. The moment she'd realized what horrible futures were possible should the virus get out, she'd come up with a myriad of theories and contingencies she'd planned to explore but had yet to develop. She would've been so much further along in her work were it not for Tom meddling with her mind, but that was in the past. It was water under the bridge, at this point.

Anna switched on the overhead light in the office, squinting while her eyes adjusted to the brightness. She peered around the messy space. It was still difficult to reconcile how such a large part of who she was had been dormant for so long. Once Jason was born, she'd been able to shut away the overachieving, workaholic geneticist who lived and breathed genetic mutations, retroviruses, and vaccine manipulations. At least now she understood why.

Anna tried to think like Dr. Wesley. That version of herself was always composed, always had a plan of action. She was methodical and strategic, a no-nonsense realist. In grad school, Anna had sworn against having children, knowing her work would always come first, that any family she had would suffer from her dedication and wholehearted addiction to science and discovering the unknown. She knew science could be callous and severe, cold and concentrated, not something that melded well with the trappings of motherhood—tenderness, compassion, selflessness. But after Tom whisked her away and she'd accidently become pregnant, everything changed.

When she heard the sound of her baby's healthy heartbeat for the first time, the innate longing to hold her child in her arms and feel the softness of its skin had been so strong—too strong to ignore. It was then that Anna knew she was mistaken to think her work could ever come first. And when she lost that baby, she'd felt a devastation unlike any other—like a piece of her had been cut away and the wound remained, gaping and open, never to be healed. But now she had Jason and Zoe, and she would outwit a thousand Gregorys to keep them safe. She just needed to focus on the task at hand.

Moving over to the standing file cabinet against the far wall, Anna crouched down, tentatively opened the bottom drawer, and searched through the papers shoved haphazardly into the back. She removed a black binder and the two files hidden beneath it. Snatching them up, she went to the desk and pushed the clutter out of the way before she sat down.

Anna's hands grew clammy as she took a deep breath and opened the binder. Finding the tab labeled MIRACLE, she flipped the divider. Her heart raced. And, as though the Dr. Wesley part of her hadn't been dormant for the past decade, she turned on the computer and began to work.

Anna's eyes burned and her head ached. The hours she'd spent staring at the computer screen—recalibrating formulas and cross-checking equations and compounds—had all but numbed her mind. Everything blurred together, and the incessant hum of the computer, what had been a comforting sound in her other life, seemed to blare in her quiet, dimly lit office. With a sigh, she raised her hands to her head, rubbing her temples in hopes of easing her headache.

She jumped at the shrill ring of the office phone. It was just after midnight, far from an acceptable hour to make a call. A shiver raked through her, chilling her to the bone. She knew better than to assume someone had the wrong number.

Anna answered the phone quickly to prevent it from ringing again. Steeling herself, she waited for the familiar, saccharine-smooth voice she knew all too well to fill her ears, hoping she was wrong. Hoping it wasn't *him*. It was too soon. She hadn't finished the neutralizer yet.

"Anna, darling," Gregory said in greeting.

Anna struggled to swallow, and her eyes flicked around the office, like he might be somewhere close by, watching. This was the moment she'd been dreading, the moment she knew would change her and her family's lives forever. This was the end of the dream. It was time to wake up.

"I'm assuming this is a good time to talk, since you're awake." *And alone,* he didn't say. "What's wrong, my dear, not sleeping well?"

Anna closed her eyes, took a silent, deep breath, then opened them again with more resolve than she felt. She forced herself to speak. "Lieutenant," she finally said. Every cell in her body screamed for her to hang up the phone, to grab the children, to drive away from their compromised location…but it was no use. She'd already considered fleeing, over and over again. Without the neutralizer, he'd eventually catch them—and he would destroy them.

"It's *General* now," Gregory purred. "But we have no need for formalities, my dear. I'm still Gregory to you. I insist."

"General?" Anna bolstered her voice. "It sounds like you've been busy."

"I have been, quite busy, actually. Of course, you would know all about it had you been here." His tone hardened. "I won't bother dredging up the past, though."

"Why are you calling, Gregory? I know you've been around my son." Her heart raced. She already knew the answer, she just hoped she could prolong the conversation long enough to figure out his plan.

As though he hadn't heard a word she'd said, he continued, "Please, catch me up on your new life with Sergeant Miller. Oh, I'm sorry, it's Tom Cartwright now, isn't it? It's only taken…" He paused like he was counting the weeks, the years. "Oh, what has it been, ten years—and the lives of many people, I might add—to find the two of you." He cleared his throat. "I guess it's partially my fault, giving you time with your family these last few years. But it's time to come home," he said easily, like she hadn't vanished in the middle of the night. "I need you. So much has changed since you left. Things are so much…better. I need you by my side."

Anna knew her situation was precarious. It would be stupid to lie to him, to pretend she wasn't in hiding—from him. Gregory knew better, knew what her feelings had been for Tom.

"What are your terms?" she asked, a void expanding inside of her.

"You're an integral part of the Great Transformation, but then I think you already know this. That's why you left, isn't it?"

She didn't need to say anything. Gregory was right.

"But, my dear, you needn't fear the unknown. Together, we're going to achieve greatness, and now that I've found you, I promise you, I will not let you go again." His threat hung suspended in their silence. When she didn't speak, he continued, "Let me give you this gift, my dear."

Anna waited with bated breath.

"I'll make it impossible for you to refuse—you'll be with me, by my side, without any guilt about leaving your family behind, and I will even let them live." He was going to force her if he had to, attempt to manipulate her mind if threatening her children didn't work.

But despite the danger, despite knowing full well that fighting him would only prolong the inevitable, she couldn't stomach the thought of leaving her children. If she gave in to Gregory, they would become a distant memory in a life so altered and grotesque from the one she'd built with Tom she might as well die.

Anna's voice was hoarse when she finally spoke again. "I can't." She hoped that by merely uttering the words she hadn't already killed her children. And when Gregory laughed bitterly, she thought maybe she had.

"The fact that you think you have a choice is amusing. I do care for you, my dear—quite deeply—but don't ever mistake my feelings for you as weakness. You *will* return to Colorado, and you *will* help me in this, Anna, or your family *will die*."

"If you think I would leave my family—" Her voice was curt and venomous, but he seemed unfazed, his laugh once again instilling a bone-chilling terror.

"I'm no fool. You won't leave your little boy and baby girl, I know this. At least not without some convincing." Fear gripped her. "Jason is getting so big. It's funny how fast they grow, isn't it? And it seems like only yesterday that Zoe was born. I like that name, by the way. It's powerful and intriguing, like her mother." Gregory paused a moment to let the weight of his words settle in.

He knew too much about her children. How long had he been watching them?

"What happens if Tom never wakes up? If Jason has an accident one day at school or while you're all out playing in the waves? That's your favorite family outing, isn't it—a day at the beach? What happens if you wake up one morning and your baby girl is gone? They're so fragile at that age…so helpless. And, now that I think about it, I haven't done much experimenting on children. I wonder what greater feats we'd achieve on younger, more malleable minds." He let out a breath, completely ignorant of her silent sobs on the other end. "I admit, the endless possibilities are troublesome, and I have no desire to hurt your children. *But*, I always get what I want, my dear, and I want you, *only* you, to come back to me. To come home."

Anna sat in her office, imagining each and every despicable thing Gregory could and would do to her family until she finally broke down and agreed to do every last thing he asked of her. She had no choice but to return to him; he'd made sure of that.

"Are you still there, darling?"

"Yes," Anna tried to say, but nothing came out. She cleared her throat. "Yes, I'm here."

"Good. Call me a sentimental fool, but I want you back, Anna, and I will torture every single person you love, slowly, if that's what it takes for you to remember where your place truly is."

Her blood ran cold and her heart felt like it was tearing apart. Tonight would be the last time she ever saw her family.

"I'm not a doctor anymore, Gregory," she admitted. "Not a scientist or a researcher. I'm not sure…I can't help you now the way I used to. I don't know—"

"No? I don't think that's true. It's still a part of you. It has to be. In fact, it's so ingrained in you that I'm sure you've been sneaking into your office the past few nights to work on your articles, to pretend you're someone else. To fight *me*." He chuckled. "I must admit, I'm a big fan of Dr. Presley's work."

Anna's insides blazed in warning and burned with fear. Was he watching her right now? She peered out the window at the juniper and cypress trees surrounding her house. She saw no one, but she felt certain that he was watching. Somehow. Some way.

Anna tried to think of some way out of this, and fast, but Gregory didn't give her the time she needed. "You have until sunrise to meet me at the docks, Anna. If you make me wait, you'll regret it," he said, his voice brusque and impatient. "Don't make me a monster. Save your family's lives and come home to me."

Anna was dead if she stayed. But it didn't matter what he did to her; he would kill her family, and that would destroy her. If she left, she'd be hollow without her family, but at least they would still be alive. Even though they would be far from her—though she would be nothing but a memory to them—she could live with herself, whatever Gregory forced her to do.

"Oh, and tell Tom he's looking a little haggard," Gregory added. The phone went dead.

Anna heard footsteps in the hallway, the floorboards creaking beneath each of Tom's lazy steps. He cleared his throat just a moment before the door creaked open.

Anna hung up the receiver.

Rubbing the scruff on the side of his face, Tom stepped into the office. "Honey, have you gotten any sleep?"

The truth—a single, simple response—barely formed on her tongue. "No, I…" She offered him a weak smile and clenched her shaking hands into fists. He couldn't know the truth, despite how desperately she wanted to tell him. "I was just working on the formula."

She rubbed her eyes and scrubbed the dread from her face, hoping a tired sigh would mask the glassy fear in her eyes. Tom wouldn't accept defeat. He wouldn't allow her to leave them behind. He would uproot them, sending them all on the run for what Anna knew would only be a matter of time before Gregory found them again—and this time he had even more reason to do something insane.

Any plan would only put them in even more danger. At least Gregory's way would spare them.

Anna had to spend the remainder of her time as a free woman working. She only had a few hours to complete the formula, in case she ever needed it. But as Tom stood there, concern filling his eyes, cracks spread throughout her heart. She would never get another night with him.

Forgetting about the formula, Anna stood and reached for him. "Let's go to bed," she said.

They headed for the bedroom, Anna walking in a panicked fog beside Tom. She jumped when his strong fingers laced with hers, a sensation so intimate and familiar that it startled her. She squeezed her eyes shut and tried to burn the feeling of his touch into her memory. How could she leave them? She blinked away fresh tears and let out a breath. The children would grow up safe and live normal lives if she left. Gregory would keep his word; it was one of his few redeeming qualities.

Tom could know nothing or he would ruin everything. The kids would need Tom alive and well, would need at least one of their parents, since they couldn't have them both.

Tom led Anna past Zoe, asleep in her cradle, and when his fingers started to slip from hers, the cracks in Anna's heart split it wide open. She loved Tom, the father of her children. The man who'd saved her and had loved her, despite knowing full well all she had done. The only person in the entire world who truly *knew* her.

She would never again feel the thick stubble of his face against her cheeks. She'd never again hear the huskiness in his voice when he whispered throaty desires into her ear. She'd never again feel his calloused hands against her skin. After tonight, she would never share his bed again. All she could do was enjoy their last night together and commit everything about him to memory. She would need these moments later, when the nights grew too dark and the days too long.

Anna pulled Tom toward her onto the mattress, drawing him in until his lips were on hers. Tom seemed confused—she'd been so angry with him earlier—but he obeyed, his body coming down over hers. He kissed her back, his desperation matching hers, and promised her all that she sought: passion—reassurance—love.

Then he pulled away, leaving panting breaths between them. Anna opened her eyes to find his gaze roaming over her face, studying her, taking her in. He was trying to understand. His brow furrowed and a pained understanding sharpened his gaze. But, when her eyes clouded with emotion, Tom's mouth found hers again. His arms were around her, and he pulled her closer, promising her all of him.

"I love you," he breathed into her ear, and each kiss vowed that he always would, no matter what. His lips brushed along the column of her neck, finding her jaw before he moved down to her collarbone. His hands, rough from sanding and gripping the wooden handles of his tools, possessed her, mind and body.

Save for the gasps and moans that escaped their lips, there were no words. And in their silence, Anna could feel the unsaid goodbye.

Anna finally fell asleep a couple hours later, naked and wrapped in Tom's arms. When she woke, the sky was already brightening. The sun would be up in another hour or so, and she needed to get to the docks. She was out of time.

Near tears, Anna peeled herself from Tom's embrace. She stood, pensive and heart breaking as she stared down at Zoe's cradle. Anna would miss her daughter's furrowed brow and shrewd, curiosity-filled eyes. She would miss Zoe's smell, the softness of her skin, and her gurgly laugh when Jason made silly, contorted faces at her.

Anna's lips pursed as she tried to picture Zoe in five years…in ten or twenty. Would she come to resemble Tom, or would she favor Anna, her hair remaining dark and her eyes that bright teal blue? What would she know about her mother? What would she think if she knew the truth? The answers shredded Anna's heart, the guilt of her past decisions telling her that she deserved every gut-wrenching emotion eating away at her.

Swallowing her sobs, Anna leaned over and stroked Zoe's angelic face with the back of her finger. Her ivory cheek. Her silky black hair. Anna closed her eyes, let out a soft, shaky breath in an attempt to calm her breathing, and straightened, creeping into her bathroom to dress without waking anyone. She would need to finish the neutralizer later, in secret. She was so close and had come too far not to finish it now. Perhaps she could use it to escape sometime down the road, or even to stop Gregory. She would need to finish it, first. Otherwise, it was just a theory.

Anna's footsteps grew slow and heavy as she crept toward the bedroom door. She paused to watch the rise and fall of her husband's chest and the way he covered his head with the pillow as he slept, just like Jason did. He was a good man, a wonderful father, and Anna knew they would all be alright without her. She wiped a stray tear from her cheek. Her leaving would hurt her more than it would hurt them. At least, she hoped that was true.

Anna pulled the bedroom door shut behind her, her hand lingering on the handle a moment longer. This part of her was fading; she could feel it with every step as she backed away.

Anna stopped outside Jason's bedroom. His door stood ajar, his small body balled up beneath his comforter. He wouldn't understand why she'd left. It would hurt him, but she willed herself to remember his strength instead. His smile. His protectiveness over his little sister. The unwavering bond he had with his father. Jason would one day be a wonderful man, she knew it deep down. And the thought of never seeing that part of him was too much. She had to go, now, before she changed her mind and sentenced them all to death.

With a choked sob, Anna covered her mouth and rushed down the stairs to the sliding glass door at the back of the house. The early morning air was frigid against her face, the damp boards of the deck turning her bare feet icy as she paced back and forth, but she didn't care. She leaned against the side of the house and cried.

She wasn't sure how long she stood there, her hands covering her face, stifling the sobs that demolished every ounce of strength she had left. Gregory was watching, she was certain, but she didn't care; there was nothing left for him to take from her. He'd won. He was getting what he wanted. Her children and husband would either hate her or forget her—both would be equal punishment and nothing worse than what she deserved.

Straightening, Anna wiped her cheeks. Crying was futile. There was no changing her mind. She needed to leave. Now. She turned to head down the porch steps.

The sliding glass door opened. “Mommy?” Jason’s small voice was thick with sleep.

Anna spun around, wiping away any remaining tears from her cheeks. Jason stood there with bleary eyes and rumpled hair, one leg of his pajama pants bunched up around his knee.

“Are you okay?” he asked, blinking.

Anna was silently thankful for the cloud cover that left little light from the brightening sky for Jason to see how swollen her face was from crying. “Of course, sweetheart.” She stepped closer to him and crouched down. “What are you doing up?” She ran her fingers through his mussed hair, looking him over to make sure he was alright. “Did you have a bad dream?” She tried to keep her voice from cracking, but it was impossible. This was the last time she would ever see her son.

“I thought I heard something, and then I couldn’t find you.” He looked around the darkened yard as if he knew the dangers that lay just out of sight.

“Well, it was probably just me fumbling over your toys. Let’s get you back inside. Okay? I don’t want you to get sick from the cold.” She lifted him into her arms, holding him tighter than necessary, silently sobbing into his shoulder as she carried him back into the safety of the house.

Once she’d put her son to bed for the final time, Anna headed back downstairs, grabbed a piece of paper and a pen, and sat down at the kitchen table. Silent tears breached her resolve and dripped down her cheeks as she wrote one last note to her husband.

Tom,

. . .

Please know that I love you very much. I've loved you since the first time I saw you. The sight of you completely crumbled my resolve to never date a military man, but your smile alone dulled every rational part of me. I'm glad it did. I'm sorry I had to leave, but please remember that it wasn't by choice. It's best if the kids never know the truth. Tell them whatever they need to hear so they never come looking for me. It's safer for them that way. We both know this. Remember, every scar makes us stronger. We have to be strong...for them. This is for the best. Love them, Tom, for the both of us, and take care of our family. I love you, all of you, always.

Yours forever,
Anna

5

DECEMBER 22, 1 AE

Having felt thousands of emotions belonging to others in the past year, you'd think I could find a word to describe how I'm feeling right now, but I can't. My mom died yesterday. I'm not sure if it's ironic or just sad that my last entry was about getting to know her.

Most people didn't like her. They didn't trust her or know her or understand her—some of my closest friends among them. And I can't say that her death has left a huge, gaping hole in my heart, because it hasn't, at least not in the way that Sanchez's mom's death left a hole in hers. It seems callous to write that, but it's true.

I feel a lot of emotions, a tumultuous combination that has had me weeping for nearly two days, but I don't think anguish is one of them. I feel sadness at losing her after only just getting her back in my life; I feel regret that I didn't say more to her or get to know her better in the short time we had together; I feel longing for the mother I'd always wanted and had come to hope she might one day be. But mostly, I just feel at a loss. It would be different if I'd lost Dani or Jason or my dad. They are my family, more than Anna Wesley ever was. Our circumstances ensured that.

But I didn't realize any of this until Sanchez sat with me today.

Although she was skeptical of my mom, I sensed a part of her that admired my mom's determination to do any and everything she could to protect her children, no matter the risks. I felt Sanchez's admiration the moment she wrapped her arms around me. Although it was a comforting gesture, it wasn't just for me, but for Sanchez, too—for her mom and the bond between mother and daughter that eluded us both, even with our very different circumstances. As she held me, I saw young Carmen Sanchez when she was her mom's keeper the way I was my dad's. I saw her when she was at her worst, before she discovered her best. And for the first time, I feel like I actually know Sanchez. And I respect her all the more for it.

"A Patrón and well whiskey," Carmen called to Sven as she sidled up to the cabana bar. "And make the whiskey a double," she added. She reveled in the slight breeze that brushed the back of her perspiring neck and across her legs. The skirt and tank top she wore did little to stave off the heat when it was muggy as hell. It certainly didn't help that she'd been on her feet for nearly eight hours without even a five-minute break.

Carmen dabbed the back of her hand against her forehead and blew a dark, wayward strand of hair out of her face. Despite the late hour, the humid Texas heat was only just abating, which meant things were just starting to get interesting in the High Roller.

Sven stepped up to the counter and flipped over two highballs. "You have that look about you—I don't like that look," he said in his thick Russian accent.

Sven had been her boss for only a few short months, so it was comical to Carmen that he thought he knew anything about her. All she knew of him was that he'd made his way to Rio Grande on a whim years ago and decided to stay for some ungodly reason, capitalizing on the poor drunkards who come out in hordes during the heat.

Carmen raised a dark eyebrow. “Yeah? And what look is that?”

“Pissed.”

“Hot,” she corrected. “Tired. You don’t give me a break, which is illegal, by the way.” Rio Grande was a hot, dirty place where loud music, late nights, and loose women were the staples for the men who frequented this part of town after most respectable folks were asleep. The hours between midnight and sunrise tended to blur, but Carmen was willing to work the worst shift possible if it meant she could bank more money faster. It was only a matter of time before she could finally get her and her mother out of this place, and she could almost taste the freedom.

“Just remember who pays your bills,” Sven muttered. “Don’t do anything stupid tonight.”

Carmen rolled her eyes at him and nodded to the drinks.

With a sidelong, warning glance, Sven scooted them closer to her on the bar. Carmen chose to ignore him, picked up the drinks, and turned her back to him. With a pleasant smile, she headed over to the two guys leaning against the standing bar on the other side of the patio. The fact that they had come to this hellhole told Carmen exactly what sort of men they were. The drunken sheen in their eyes was to be expected now that High Roller was nearing its late-night last call. *Nothing like riled-up, overstimulated scumbags to finish the night off,* she thought as she hinged her false smile in place.

“There she is,” the taller, goateed ingrate drawled. He winked at Carmen as she took the Patrón off her drink tray and handed it to him.

“That will be sixteen fifty for both,” she said, hoping her big smile and painted red lips would earn her a decent tip. They could stare and hoot and catcall her, as long as they didn’t touch. That was her deal with Sven.

Goatee man reached for his drink, and the instant his clammy thumb deliberately brushed the back of her hand, her smile faltered, taking any remaining patience with it.

"Ain't you a sexy thing," he said with another wink, his buddy grinning beside him.

Carmen pulled her hand from his, a warning in her glare. "Sixteen fifty," she repeated flatly and placed the drinks back on the tray.

Goatee leaned in a little, his eyelids closing slowly before they flitted back open again, making Carmen wonder if he wasn't just drunk but on something. "When're you off, sweet cheeks?"

"I'm afraid that's not in the cards," she said, holding her hand out for payment.

"Come on, don't be like that—"

With aching feet and zero patience, Carmen took a step back. "Do you want your damn drinks or not? No money, no drinks."

With a laugh, Goatee reached into his pocket and pulled out his wallet. He fumbled with it for a few seconds before he could get out a twenty-dollar bill. Flashing her another sick smile, he held it out to her.

Carmen assumed she was stepping into a trap the moment she reached for the twenty, but she had little choice. The moment she did, the man wrapped his hand around her wrist and tugged her toward him, the drinks on her serving tray sloshing over the rim of their glasses.

"Why don't you join me and Paulie here for a nightcap, sweet cheeks?" Goatee's voice held less of a question and more of a demand. He eyed her up and down, blatant lust in his eyes.

Had she had fangs, Carmen would've bared them at that moment, but she could only smile. "Let go of me," she stated coolly. "Now."

Paulie hooted, goading his friend on. "She just shot you down, Danny Boy." He hit his friend on the back. "Flat-out *denied.*"

Danny Boy didn't like that. His lip pulled up into a snarl and he shook his head. "Not everyone can handle Big Dan," he said, as if she were missing out on the best time of her life.

"No doubt," Carmen muttered and snatched the cash from his hand. She set the two highballs on the cocktail table and turned to head back to the bar.

One of the men smacked her on the ass, then squeezed.

Before she could think about it, she slapped Danny Boy's hand away and reached out, grabbing him by the balls and backing him up against the railing. Paulie choked with awe and laughter as he took a stumbling step backward.

"Ah!" Danny Boy winced and hunched over. "You stupid bitch—"

"Didn't your mamá ever teach you how to talk to a lady?" she growled. "Touch me again and I'll break your face."

"Sanchez!" Sven shouted from the bar, hurrying over to them.

She clutched Danny Boy's balls harder and turned her wrist, earning a gasp.

"God damn it, Carmen!" Sven yelled. "That's it!"

Carmen's heart hammered in her chest. She was done for, she knew it. But damn it, it was worth it. With one final squeeze, she let go of Danny Boy's balls, straightened, and took a step back.

"That stupid bitch—"

"You're done!" Sven shouted, arms flailing. "Get your shit and get out of here."

"Fine with me," she said, sticking the cash into her bra. "This is bullshit." With a dramatic tug, she pulled off her apron and tossed it at Sven. "I'll be in tomorrow for my check."

The whole way home, Carmen's thoughts raced, her bloodstream flooding with adrenaline. She felt relief, sure, but also the daunting pressure to find a replacement income equal to what she'd been making at the bar—a thousand bucks every two weeks. Aside from living expenses, she still had her father's debts to pay off—for the time being—and a trip anywhere but here with her mother, Maria, to fund. And this time, she knew her mother was serious about leaving her father and their twenty-five years of dysfunction.

Maria Sanchez was, in many ways, a strong woman. But when it came to her husband, Carlos, the ex-bullfighter, drunk, and chauvinistic pig extraordinaire, Maria hadn't a single vertebra in her backbone. She'd never been independent; she'd never had the choice, since she'd been married off at the age of seventeen. But no more. With Carmen's encouragement, she was ready to leave, to strike out on her own, to finally *live* her own life.

Carmen turned down the dirt drive and headed toward the acre of overgrown weeds that housed their dilapidated two-bedroom ranch home. The moment she pulled her old jalopy into the driveway, she knew something wasn't right. It was nearly three in the morning, and the lights were on inside, the front door open.

"Oh, Mamá," Carmen breathed and pushed her car door open with the creak and groan of rusty metal. "Mamá?" she called tentatively, slamming the car door shut.

She hurried through the open front door to find the interior of the house in shambles. Broken picture frames lay fractured on the floor, and the furniture was overturned. Her mother sat on the couch, face puffy and tear-streaked as she stared at the broken box television.

"He came back," Carmen said absently and hurried to her mother's side. She searched her mother's face, then frantically scanned her body, making sure she wasn't hurt worse than the red palm print on her cheek.

Maria stared beyond Carmen at nothing, barely blinking. She was spiraling into a black hole of regret and self-blame that would take weeks for her to climb back out from. Carmen had seen it happen far too often, and she hated this part of the abuse, even more than the bruises and the fear. Her mother's suffering was Carmen's undoing. Each and every time.

"Mamá," she breathed. "What did he want this time? Money?"

Maria stared ahead, though her chin inclined ever so slightly.

"Did you give it to him?" Carmen wished more than believed that, for once in her life, her mother had had the courage to say no to her father. "Mamá?"

Maria shook her head, surprising her daughter.

"You didn't give it to him?"

"He knew where to find it," she admitted, her voice only a whisper. And Carmen knew her father's greedy ways well enough to know that he'd taken every cent, again. Her mother refused to put anything in a bank, said that she didn't trust them, but Carmen knew the real reason for it.

"Let me guess," Carmen said, "it wasn't enough." By the state the house was in, that much was obvious.

"He thought I was hiding more from him," Maria said with a faraway look in her eyes. "He knows there is more hidden away somewhere."

"And he'll never get it," Carmen said. She, at least, kept her portion of their escape fund stowed safely in a hiding spot under the floorboards, somewhere her father would never find it and her mother wouldn't think to look, if he'd ever threatened her for it. "That's why you should've put what you had in the bank, Mamá. Now we'll never get out of this fucking place." Carmen let her head hang as she took deep breaths.

Her mother would be the death of her, she knew it. Carmen had resented not having siblings growing up, that there was no one to share the burden of this lot she'd been given. But now, after all this time, she was grateful there was no one else for her father to lash out at. No one else to suffer like she and her mother had. No one else for her to worry about.

Carmen was tired of this, tired of seeing her mother reduced to this weak and pathetic woman. She was sick and tired of living in fear and poverty and rage. She wanted more, for both of them.

Carmen shook her head. She was just so tired. "You should've called me," she said, brushing her mother's gray-streaked black hair from her face.

Maria slowly turned her face to Carmen, her full lips split and bloodied.

"Mamá, I didn't take all those self-defense courses for nothing. I could've helped you—I could've protected you. That's why I bought you that cell phone. That's why my number is programmed in there...why Tía's number is in there."

Maria tried to smile, but her lips only twitched in the corner, her chin trembling. She'd been beautiful, in another life, but her youth was long shadowed by decades of fear and depression and everything in between.

"You were working," Maria finally said. "We need the money. I can handle your father until—"

"No, Mamá, you can't." Carmen stood up, unable to control the rage of twenty-three years of the same old bullshit bubbling up inside of her. "When will it be too much?" She threw her hands up and began to pace.

"He's your father—"

"No," Carmen said adamantly, "he's an abusive son of a bitch who hasn't been my father for a *very* long time. When will you see that he is going to *kill* you someday?"

"He's still my husband!" Maria screeched, eyes bleary with pain and fear—fear he might return, but even more fear that he never would.

"He's poison! He's sucking the life out of you, and this stops now." She held her breath for a minute, weighing their options. It would be tight, and far from comfortable, but they could do it. "We're leaving," she said, those two words hanging in the air like the ring of a gong.

Carmen stomped out of the living room, stepping over an overturned bookshelf in the hallway as she made her way to her bedroom. Everything was torn apart in her room as well, and Carmen prayed her father hadn't found her money stash under the floorboards of her closet. With a smile, she silently thanked God when she noticed the boards still in place. She pulled up the loose floor and reached in for the tin box her grandfather had given her. Relief filled her, tears springing in her eyes, when her fingertips brushed the cool metal.

"Save your money," her abuelo had told her the day he handed her the metal bin, a dozen silver dollars clinking around inside. *"Save your money, and one day, niña, you will be able to get away from this place."* He'd said it as if he'd foreseen this moment. Even at ten years old, Carmen had known he was right.

"Mamá," Carmen called again. "Vámonos. Grab a bag. We're going to Tía Lucia's." It wasn't the ideal plan, but it was all she had right now. *It's now or never,* Carmen told herself as she pulled a duffel bag out from underneath her bed and started mindlessly stuffing it with clothes. "Pack some things. We're going tonight." After all, other than the waitressing gig she had four days a week, there was nothing but her mother keeping her in this godforsaken town, and Tía Lucia had been urging them to leave the old farmhouse for years. *"There's nothing keeping you there—nothing but him."*

With a bag filled with random clothing, Carmen rushed back into the living room to find her mother still sitting on the couch. She was staring at nothing, eyes glazed over and a lone tear trickling down her cheek.

"Mamá," Carmen whispered. "Please, listen to me."

Whether it was the supplication in Carmen's voice or a sudden moment of clarity, after a few heartbeats, Maria looked at her daughter.

"Please, Mamá," Carmen pleaded. "I can't stay here a moment longer. I know you're scared, but *you* can't stay here, either. Not knowing when he's going to come back—what he's going to take. What he'll do…" Tears pricked Carmen's eyes as she realized how truly desperate she was for her mother to simply listen. "Please, Mamá…do this *for me.*"

Maria's eyebrows rose, and her eyes widened in a look of understanding. She offered Carmen a small, hesitant smile and reached her hand out to cup her daughter's cheek. Her smile widened a little and she leaned in and kissed the side of Carmen's cheek. "I love you, mija."

"Mamá," Carmen uttered with another plea. "You *must* leave this place. We'll go together—you and me."

Maria took in the urgency in her daughter's eyes. It was like she was finally seeing what she'd done to her daughter—the position she'd put her in for all these years.

Carmen watched with bated breath as something clicked in her mother, and she knew that she'd finally broken through to her. Leaving wasn't just some far-off thing they talked about, not anymore. Leaving was happening. Now.

"You have your father's eyes. They were kind once," Maria said, though Carmen wondered if her mother was trying to convince herself of the memory. "And you have his stubbornness—he is why you are so strong." She exhaled a sad laugh. "Even if you can't see it, I can." Carmen wasn't sure why her mother was telling her this, but she didn't care as long as it led to her getting up and packing a bag.

Carmen held her hand out to her mother. "Come on, Mamá."

Maria leaned forward to stand, wiping the moisture from her eyes.

Carmen jumped to her feet, almost too hopeful to breathe.

"I'm sorry I've brought this on us, mija. You are a good girl—you are so much stronger than I could ever be."

"It's not too late, Mamá. We'll go to Tía's. You'll be safe there. She misses you, remember? She loves you and wants to see you."

Her mother's brow furrowed and she titled her head slightly. "What about you?"

Carmen swallowed. "Me too, Mamá," she said. *At least, for now.*

Two weeks passed relatively calmly. One morning, Carmen was sitting with her mother, her aunt, and her uncle in the breakfast nook of their home in Houston, eating homemade tamales. Their neighborhood was so nice compared to the one Carmen had grown up in—new homes with air conditioning and big lots that backed up to a meadow extending all the way to the hills. To Carmen, her aunt's house felt like a home—someone *else's* home, but a home nonetheless—and she was grateful for it.

Unlike Carmen, her cousins had gone off to college. The eldest, Jamie, had already graduated from the University of Texas and was married with a baby on the way. Sleeping in Jamie's old room was a daily reminder of what Carmen had never had, the sort of life and family she'd missed out on growing up. It showed her what she wanted to do with the years ahead of her and confirmed what she never wanted to do again: give in.

There had been no word from her father, which was a saving grace. Carmen knew her mother would be safe in Houston, living with family Carmen wasn't sure her father would even remember existed. Maria had pushed them all away years ago, the way she was pushing her beans and tamales around on her plate now. She wouldn't eat much, Carmen knew, but she held onto the hope that a couple more weeks was all it would take to bring her mother back to life; months from now, her mother would understand why they'd had to leave. Perhaps she would even be grateful.

Silence hung heavy in the air. Awkward smiles were exchanged. They all watched Maria out of the corners of their eyes, wondering if this was the moment she would finally break.

"So," her Aunt Lucia said brightly, "how is job-hunting going?"

Carmen glanced from her aunt to her uncle, Tony. He nodded for Carmen to tell them, but she took a large bite of breakfast instead. "It's going," she finally answered after swallowing, then took a sip of her sweet tea. "I'm still trying to decide what I want to do exactly."

Lucia cleared her throat and twirled the diamond ring around on her finger. "Did you talk to my friend Barbara at the restaurant?"

Carmen nodded. "Yes—well, I tried. She wasn't there when I went in yesterday, but I'll try again today."

With a nod, Lucia took a sip from her glass, and Carmen could tell her aunt was trying to think of other friends that might owe her a favor.

"Really," Carmen said, "please don't worry about me. I don't want you to have to pull any strings. It would make me uncomfortable." Besides, Carmen had other plans—plans that didn't involve waiting tables or any other form of customer service.

When Tony cleared his throat, Carmen couldn't bring herself to look at him. Instead, she watched her mother, who was still staring down at her plate. Carmen hated to leave her, especially like this, but she'd made up her mind. Her uncle had helped her make the decision, and she felt empowered by it. That was how she knew it was the right thing to do.

"Mamá," Carmen said, reaching out to take her mother's hand. "I'm considering a career in the army."

Maria finally drew her gaze up and met her daughter's eyes. She looked confused. Frightened, even.

"Oh?" Lucia said. "I see."

Carmen met her aunt's gaze, then her uncle's.

Tony offered her a wink and dipped his head, hiding a smile.

"You knew about this, Anthony?" his wife asked, her eyebrows raised.

"Carmen deserves to be off on her own," he said with an ease that was music to Carmen's ears. She'd been considering enlisting for years, and she felt guilty for making the decision without consulting her mother, but now, with her uncle in her corner and her mother safe, she had the strength to do it.

Carmen balled up her napkin and placed it on the table. "They would provide me with room and board and money of my own that I can send to you. I'd be trained—have a specialty—and I'd be able to travel." She smiled, hope chasing away the uncertainty. "It would be a whole new life."

Tony scraped up the last bite of his breakfast from his plate. "We're going to the recruitment office tomorrow, if either of you care to join us."

Tears filled Maria's eyes, though she said nothing. Carmen's heart sank as the relief of finally getting this huge announcement off of her chest was consumed by guilt in leaving her mother behind and alone. *But she won't be alone,* she reminded herself. "It's just to get information, Mamá. I'm not leaving tomorrow or anything."

"Besides, Maria, you have us now," Lucia said, giving her sister's forearm a squeeze. "It will give us an opportunity to make up for lost time."

Maria offered her sister a resolved but weak smile, then looked at her daughter. "You've wanted this for a long time, mija," she said.

Carmen's eyes opened wide. She hadn't known her mother paid enough attention to her to figure it out.

"I saw the brochures in your room. I thought it was a phase." Maria's eyes filled with a sadness so acute that Carmen could nearly feel it in her soul. "You have stayed in a place you hate all this time—for me—something you should never have had to do. I understand."

"If I didn't know you would be safe," Carmen added, "I'd never even—"

"I know, mija," Maria said with a nod. She reached out a hand, taking her daughter's chin in her fingers. "You should do this," she said, surprising Carmen. "You will do good things."

Unable to resist, Carmen leaned in and wrapped her arms around her mother.

"You will do good things," her mother repeated, almost to herself. "I know you will."

"Number four fifty-three," a woman's sharp voice rang out through the silent waiting room. Dozens of men and women, mostly in their teens and some in their early twenties, like Carmen, filled the room. All of them waited their turn for shots, ID cards, and eye exams. After four hours of listening to one number called after another, the numbers all began to sound the same to Carmen.

"Number four-five-three!" the woman called again, more of a shout this time.

The dark-skinned island boy sitting beside Carmen nudged her shoulder. When she looked at him, her eyes heavy with the exhaustion of boredom, he nodded down at the tiny slip of paper with her number crumpled in her hand. He flashed her a wide, toothy grin. "Looks like you're up," he said, waggling his eyebrows at her.

"Oh. Shit." Carmen jumped to her feet. "Thanks," she said over her shoulder. She hurried toward the uniformed woman who was eye-scolding her, trying not to yawn as she passed her, and stepped into a compact photo room.

The female officer extended her hand and nodded to the folder of papers Carmen was holding. "Your form?"

Gathering her wits about her, Carmen rifled through the documents, pulling out the sheet containing her personal identification information.

"Sanchez, Carmen," the woman read aloud, speaking to herself. She nodded to the blue boot outlines painted on the cement floor nearby. "Stand over there, please."

The woman gave Carmen a few directives and there were flashes of light. After a few more minutes, Carmen was exiting the room with the instructions to wait for her final round of shots before chow time in twelve hundred hours.

As Carmen made her way to her seat, she wondered if she'd ever been so exhausted and bored. It had been over twenty-four hours since she arrived at Fort Sill Army Base in Lawton, Oklahoma, for testing and processing before basic training. By the end of tomorrow, she would know what the next chapter of her life would look like—or at least have a better idea than she did now—and the thought both thrilled and terrified her, even in her exhausted state.

With a sigh, Carmen took her seat again, remembering her mother's sad eyes and supportive words when Carmen officially signed the papers, making the commitment to enlist. Her future no longer seemed so bleak, though you'd never guess that from her mother's expression when they said their goodbyes. Carmen couldn't shake that old familiar incessant worry she'd always had for her mother.

"They couldn't have waited for us to be bright-eyed and bushy-tailed, could they?" the guy beside her said.

Carmen glanced at him. His smile was warm, but she was wary of the twinkle in his eyes.

"They wait until we've been waiting here for hours," he continued, "sitting in our own stench, to take our photos."

Carmen cracked a smile. "Seriously." With a sigh, she leaned back in her chair, crossing her arms over her chest, subconsciously mirroring his relaxed pose. "Thanks for the nudge earlier," she said. "Really."

"No problem." He extended his hand. "I'm Dustin Harper."

She shook his hand. "Carmen Sanchez."

After a few weeks of drill after drill, Carmen found her stride. She already felt like a new person. She was Sanchez, the stubborn one—or so the drill sergeant called her, though she never once disobeyed him. An afternoon spent puking outside the gas chamber, followed by a day of running to the brink of passing out, helped Sanchez learn to anticipate the struggles of the day. She came to embrace every challenge. Exhaustion sucked, but it didn't matter, not when her sore muscles made her feel more alive than she'd ever felt in her life.

Sanchez didn't speak much to her new peers, save for the nights she was on fireguard with Harper, patrolling the housing quarters and cleaning. All they longed for after a long day like that was sleep, but Harper could easily fill the silence with stories to keep them alert. Carmen found herself strangely grateful, discovering comfort in his friendly demeanor.

"So," Dustin said as he marched through the barracks hallway beside Sanchez. He was clearly bored out of his mind. "If we were in another life, not here, on duty, what would a no-nonsense *chica* like you be doing right now?" He waggled his always-dancing eyebrows at her. Had she not puked on him, learned how to shoot alongside him, and come to trust him more than she'd ever trusted anyone else, she would've been offended by this not-so-subtle come-on.

"Nothing that would've involved you," she said dryly and clasped her hands behind her back.

Harper's grin widened in response. "If I didn't already know you liked me, that would've been a blow to my ego."

"Darn," she said, and they turned down another hallway, walking side by side through the labyrinth, glancing in the barracks and listening for any disruptions within the rooms.

"Seriously, though, Sanchez. I know you're a badass now and all—at least you *think* you are—but you haven't always been like this, right? What did you used to do for fun? And don't say *nothing*," he said before she could answer him. "You always say *nothing*, and nothing is boring. I need titillating conversation if I'm going to make it through the next thirty minutes."

Sanchez looked at him askance, trying to decide how to answer.

"Well?" His brows rose with anticipation. "You know all about me. I'm an open book…"

"Unfortunately," she muttered.

"…and I know almost nothing about you. So come on, spill the beans. Give me the lowdown on your life before."

Sanchez lifted her shoulders defensively. "What exactly do you want to know? I didn't leave a boyfriend behind. I have no kids. My father is not in the picture. My mother is in Houston—"

"Tell me something no one else knows," he said easily. "Something that feels out of your comfort zone."

Sanchez frowned.

"I'm serious. I'm supposed to trust you with my life and I know absolutely nothing about you, other than that you hate French toast—even though you never complain—and you're waiting for someone to send you a letter that hasn't come yet, and you're seriously more badass than any of us jocks and macho men on the squad."

Surprised, Sanchez frowned at him. "How did you know about the French toast?"

With a deep breath, Harper looked at her. "That face you're making right now—that face—that's what your face does when you're perplexed or grossed out. It's the only emotion I've picked up on from you, and it's a pretty obvious one."

That made her smile, even if it was just a little slip of one. "Ah, I see. Well, I don't like French toast because it's too sweet…and I've been waiting for a letter from my mom. I've written her a few times now, but I haven't heard anything from her since I got here."

When Harper didn't say anything, Sanchez looked at him. His gaze was fixed on the floor in front of them, his eyebrows pinched together. "You left on bad terms?" he asked.

Sanchez shook her head, and they turned around to return the way they'd come. "Not exactly."

"Then," he started again, "you're worried about her? Why?"

Sanchez wanted to act indifferent about his question, but she found it difficult to put up any sort of front when Harper was looking at her so intently. She trusted him; she *wanted* to confide in him. She'd never felt anything like that before. Finally, she met Harper's gaze, and the sincere curiosity in his eyes allowed the truth to fall from her lips. "I'm worried my dad might've found her."

Harper stopped walking, jaw set. "What do you mean, *found* her?"

"He's not a good guy—he never has been. And she's never been without him. I'm worried that she's so dependent on him, no matter how he treats her, that either she called him and he came for her, or he found her and did something…God, it makes me sick to even think about." Sanchez cleared her throat. "Either way, the longer she's silent, the more I question coming here."

"Does she have anyone else to look out for her?"

"I left her with my aunt and uncle," Carmen said, her chest tightening. What if it had been a mistake? "I received a message from them a couple weeks ago, but they only said she was okay, that's it. And that was weeks ago."

"Then I'm sure she's fine and your family is taking care of her." Sanchez imagined Harper was speaking to her the way he would one of his sisters. He nudged her shoulder. "If your mother is as stubborn as mine, she's going to do what she wants, regardless of how much you disagree or worry. Besides, she's an adult, and you can't control her. I know I can't control my mother, no matter how much I try." He laughed to himself and shook his head. "I'm sure she'll write soon. You're probably worrying for nothing."

Deep down, Sanchez knew Harper was right. She was so used to worrying she wasn't sure she knew how to stop, especially now that her mother was over four hundred miles away from her.

When the mail finally came, so did a letter for Private Carmen Sanchez, Battery Battalion of the Fourth Platoon. It was from Lucia, and a wave of dread washed over Sanchez as Private Billings handed it to her.

Holding her breath, Sanchez hurried over to her bunk, seated herself, and tore the top of her envelope open. Carefully, she began to read:

Niña, lo siento, pero tu madre es muerte. She died last week, and I wasn't sure how to tell you. A letter didn't seem appropriate, but I didn't know what else to do. After you left, she stopped coming out of her room. I thought your letters would make her feel better after a time, but I was wrong. She went for a walk around the block last Monday but didn't come back. We searched for her for two days and finally found her at your old house. We don't know if he hurt her or she did it to herself, but both her and your father's bodies were there.

Carmen, I'm so sorry I lied to you. I've included the letter we found in her room, though I—

Carmen dropped her aunt's letter and gripped her mother's with shaking fingers. Her eyes filled with tears, her heart thumping and lungs gasping for air so quickly that she began to feel lightheaded.

My beautiful mija. I've been thinking a lot lately. I know it is my job to support you and care for you, yet you have always done this for me instead.

As Carmen read the words, disbelief and anger and regret roared so loudly she didn't know what to think.

. . .

With you gone, I've found a strange sense of peace. I know what I want now, what I've always wanted but was too afraid to accept. But you are gone, and you are living your own life. It's time for me to face my own.

Carmen's tears blotted the page and her eyes blurred, forcing her to wipe them away so she could see.

I love you, mija, and I'm sorry for everything. I wish I could be the mother you deserve, especially when you didn't have a father you could love. But I am so very proud of you. You are so strong and courageous, more than I should've ever asked or expected you to be.

Be you, my darling girl, always. You are important.—Tu madre

Hands shaking, Carmen crumpled the letter in her fist and rose to her feet. The guilt. Regret. Anger. It filled her eyes, clouded her mind, and weighed heavy in her heart.

"There she is—Sanchez?" Harper stopped beside her bunk, but she barely registered his presence.

Crying out, she threw the crumpled letter against the wall. She felt numb and disbelieving as her mother's final written words blared over and over in her head: You are important. *But not enough to live for,* she thought. Never enough to live for, to fight for. *Never enough.*

"Sanchez?" Harper said carefully, and he reached out for her. "Is it your mom?

Is she okay?" He took hold of Carmen's arms, firmly but gently. "Look at me, Baby Girl," Harper said. "Look at me…"

Oblivious to the drill sergeant, Biggs, and a few others watching nearby, Carmen looked at Harper. He was a point of stability, a calming voice. She blinked and his reassuring green eyes came into focus through her tears. Then she leaned into him, crying in his arms.

She wept for the mother who she'd tried, however impossibly, to save, and for the future she was strangely grateful to have. "She's all I had," Carmen said, her own words surprising her.

"No, she's not," he whispered, tightening his hold on her. "You've got me, too."

6

JANUARY 1, 2 AE

Yesterday, after Camille, Becca, Peter, and Mase constructed the most amazing metallic tree up on the hill behind the farmhouse, Jake told me about Harper's vision of Chris having his baby. It all makes sense now, Harper's strange behavior and distraction these past few days. I thought it might've been about Dani's pregnancy, but it was much more personal than that.

I thought the idea of Harper and Chris having children together was exciting to think about at first, but on my way to bed after the New Year's festivities early this morning, I overheard Harper tell Chris about his prophecy. Although he was filled with hope and excitement, I could also feel Chris's remorse. She was thinking of her twin boys, who died from the Virus. She was thinking about her ex-husband, Mark, and how things ended with him. How she'd wished he would die, and he did.

Chris is a good woman, a strong woman. She's also haunted by the things she said and did out of anger in her life before, which is a side of her no one knows about or ever sees. I know the burden she carries for wishing her ex-husband dead, even if she isn't the one who killed him. The Virus killed him, just like it took her boys from her. She didn't curse him, no matter what she thinks or how she feels, and I wish, more than anything, that I could tell her that. But to do that, I'd have to admit that I know her secrets. That I've seen her most regretful moments.

It's days like this, when I see private things and I want to offer some semblance of comfort but can't, that I need to write.

"I'm two seconds away from losing it, Chris." Mark's voice was sharp, hoarse, his posture rigid, his eyes bloodshot. The sound of a baby's screeching wails penetrating their bedroom wall had become his own personal nails on a chalkboard. He was beyond exhausted—they both were. Chris thought that two seconds from losing it was maybe an overly generous estimate, in his case. The North Carolina heat wasn't helping matters either.

"But," Chris said, "the books say consistency is essential with sleep training."

"I don't care what the books say, Chris." His chest rose and fell as he took a deep, shaky breath. "I haven't slept through the night since they were born. This sleep-training crap isn't working."

Chris raised her hands in a useless attempt to soothe her husband. "It takes time. I told you—"

Mark stared at Chris for a few seconds, his features softening. Chris thought he might relent; it was what would be best for the twins, after all. Finally, he blew out a breath and shook his head. "I can't do this again tonight, Chris," he said, desperation filling his eyes. "I just can't…" He ran his fingers through his hair, making the short, dark strands stand on end. "I have an early morning. Please, just *shut them up*."

With those final three words—*shut them up*—Chris got over the urge to play peacemaker in the relationship. Now she wanted to punch Mark. She faced off with him from across the bed, fists on her hips. Her jaw creaked she was clenching it so tightly, and she breathed in and out through flared nostrils. She couldn't risk opening her mouth to speak; if she did, she'd curse Mark up one side of hell and down the other. And then she really, truly might punch him.

Sure, she'd agreed to bear the brunt of the parenting responsibilities; it had been the only way to convince Mark that the time for making babies was upon them. But that also meant she called the shots when it came to raising them, and that included deciding to sleep train them this way. *Her* decision. *Her* responsibility. *Her* fucking call, dammit.

"I swear to God, Chris…" Mark had never, not once, looked at Chris the way he was looking at her now. Like he loathed her. Like the sight of her filled him with rage. Like she was just another one of the women he couldn't stand, rather than the one he had sworn, over and over, was so different. The one he couldn't live without. The only one he would ever consider having kids with. The one who was special, who he would love forever, no matter what.

Mark's gaze was far from loving now. Chris snorted bitterly and shook her head. What a romantic crock of shit. She trudged to the bedroom door, yanked it open, and passed through without a backward glance. If Mark wanted to shut the door to dull the noise, he could do it his own damn self.

Tomorrow night. Tomorrow she'd stick to her guns, regardless of the death glares and hatred Mark tossed her way. But tonight, she was too tired. For five weeks, ever since the boys were born, she'd been too tired. She loved them with all her heart, but she couldn't help but wonder if having them had been a mistake. Maybe they were soaking up all of her love until she had nothing left to give to Mark anymore.

Sometimes, especially on nights like this, Chris felt like she'd sacrificed her relationship with her husband so she could have kids, and she wasn't entirely sure she would make the same choice again if given the chance to do it over.

Exhaustion and fear knotted up around Chris's heart, her irritation spiking as she slipped into the boys' room. She'd decorated the nursery with soothing blues and greens and wall decals of cartoonish jungle animals. But now, the sight of those shadowed, playful animals made her want to scream.

She and Mark had a good thing going—a great thing, back when it had been just the two of them. They'd only had minor issues before; their only big "fight" had been about having kids in the first place. Mark had changed his mind from what he'd said when they first got together, and now he wasn't sure he wanted kids anymore. Chris had reminded him—with ever-diminishing patience—that kids had been part of the deal. That had almost destroyed them; probably would have if Mark hadn't relented.

Maybe it destroyed us anyway, Chris thought, and she mourned the loss of the near-perfect partnership she and Mark had shared… once. It felt like such a long time ago now.

Reluctantly, Chris reached into the crib on the left side of the room and lifted the swaddled baby from the mattress. "Shhhhh, baby boy," she murmured to little Alex, who was mindlessly wailing the night away. Just the one crier tonight, thankfully.

The strips of light streaming in through the blinds from the streetlight out front illuminated Alex's pudgy face, pinched and beet red. The second he was cozied against Chris's shoulder, his cries quieted to sniffles and hiccups.

Chris walked over to the other crib and peered down at little Benjamin. She'd assumed he was still asleep, considering his quiet state, but his eyes were open and fixed on her. There was an ocean of innocence in those eyes. Innocence and understanding and wisdom and love, a combination that she knew all too well from her own childhood would flee after years of listening to her and Mark fight.

"It's not your fault, baby boy," Chris said, reaching into the crib with one hand to stroke his cherub cheek with the back of her finger. She was inundated with guilt at her earlier thoughts that either of her precious boys was a mistake. What she and Mark had shared as a childless couple paled in comparison to what she had with her baby boys. Whatever happened between her and Mark, Alex and Benji were more than worth it.

Chris swallowed back tears and cleared her throat. "We'll get through this," she vowed. For the boys. For the people she and Mark used to be. For the family she knew they could be.

They would work it out.

Chris paced in the hallway, just outside the boys' room, staring at her phone. Five till six. Mark should've been home by now. In fact, he should've been home fifteen minutes ago. He'd worked the graveyard shift at Fort Bragg's hospital last night—not his usual shift—and the only reason Chris hadn't arranged for a sitter for this morning was because he'd promised to be home by the time she had to leave for PT.

But the boys were both sick with the flu—a dangerous thing considering they were barely nine months old—and she wasn't willing to leave her babies unattended for even a minute. If their fevers spiked any higher, they'd be in the brain damage danger zone and would require an immediate trip to the hospital. Especially since the baby aspirin she'd given them an hour ago wasn't making a dent in their slowly rising temperatures.

Another minute ticked by, then another.

Chris tapped the button to call Mark for the seventh time and brought the phone up to her ear, blowing out a heavy sigh. Her CO would chew her out for being late—again—and the guys would give her a hard time for letting her "mommy problems" get in the way of her doing her job, but they would get over it, eventually. So long as she took responsibility and accepted their heckling. So long as she manned up when Mark didn't seem able to.

At the sound of the garage door opening, Chris ended the unanswered call and headed up the hall and through the living room to the kitchen to stare at the door to the garage. She heard Mark walk past the door into the house, open and shut the garage fridge they kept stocked with bottles of water, beer, and soda, and ascend the three wooden steps that led to the house. Or, rather, stomp up them. She crossed her arms over her chest.

Mark flung the door open, and he already had the can of beer up to his mouth by the time he came into sight. At six in the God damn morning. Memories of her drunken father flashed through Chris's mind, and she barely reined in her spike of annoyance.

When Mark's eyes met Chris's, she raised her eyebrows pointedly.

"Ah, shit, babe…" Mark lowered the can and set it on the nearest patch of kitchen counter. "I totally forgot you had PT this morning."

Chris closed her eyes and breathed in and out through her nose, deep and slow. Mark had been trying to take a more active role in raising their boys—in being her true partner—she knew it. These past few days, with the boys being so sick, he'd even stayed up and held them through the night with Chris. The effort was there, but then small things like this would crop up, reminding her that his heart wasn't in it.

Opening her eyes, Chris unclenched her jaw and focused on Mark's face. Dark half-moons shadowed his eyes, and his skin had a sallow tint. She wondered if he was catching whatever the twins had or if he'd just had an exceptionally exhausting day. She wondered if difficulties at work were the reason he was suddenly doing a damn good impersonation of her father. She wondered, but in her present state of irritation, she didn't really care.

"Their temperatures haven't come down at all," Chris said, turning her back to Mark. She grabbed the video monitor off the counter and handed it to him. "Check them every ten minutes, sooner if they start fussing. It could mean their fevers are worse."

"I know."

She stopped beside him, meeting his eyes. "If they go over 104, take them in."

"I *know*, Chris. I'm a nurse, remember?"

With a sniff, she brushed past him, heading for the door to the garage.

"Chris."

She paused at the door, hand gripping the knob.

"It's not my fault—me being late."

Chris squeezed the cool metal, like she could channel her anger into the inanimate object rather than lash out at her husband. "What, did somebody else forget for you?"

"It was a busy night," he snapped. "We had two deaths, and one flatline right at the end of my shift—a kid. We managed to bring her back, but if I'd left any earlier…"

Chris bowed her head, biting her tongue. She took another of those slow, deep breaths. "I'm sorry you had a hard night," she said quietly on her exhale. *But our kids should come first,* she didn't say. Couldn't say. Would never say. "I'll come straight back so you can get some rest."

"They're napping," Chris said from the couch as Mark walked in from the garage. Apparently, she didn't say it soon enough, because Mark failed to catch the door as it swung closed, slamming like it always did unless eased shut. Chris cringed at the sound and glanced at the baby monitor, holding her breath for the impending, overdramatic cries of her two very toddlery boys.

Thankfully, the baby monitor remained silent, the screen black.

"I'd like a nap," Mark grumbled without even glancing at Chris. He held two tall cans of beer in his left hand, one stacked on top of the other. His drinking was a constant irritant in their relationship, but no matter how many times or different ways Chris pleaded with him to cut back—to not make her and their boys watch him slowly kill himself with alcohol like her father had—Mark continued on.

Chris set her book down on the couch cushion beside her and pulled her legs up, hugging them to her chest. "Then take one," she said, thinking that Mark quiet, asleep, and, later, well rested, would be better than the overly loud, unsteady man he would be in a few hours if he spent his afternoon in the usual way. Besides, she had some news that would be best delivered to a sober Mark rather than the unpredictable person he became after his afternoon six-pack.

"But then you'd be on your own with the boys," Mark said. He stopped behind the couch and leaned over Chris, planting a kiss on the top of her head. "Can't have that, now can we?"

Chris smiled up at her husband, heart thudding in her chest. It couldn't wait, then. She had to tell him now, while his mind and emotions were still clear. "Sit with me," she said, patting the open space beside her on the couch. "I want to talk to you about something."

Mark tilted his head to the side, eyes narrowed. Slowly, he rounded the end of the couch and sank down. He set the bottom can of beer on the hardwood floor, then cracked open the top one and took a long drag before looking at Chris. That wary stare told her he was anticipating a rehashing of the drinking debate.

"I got a call this morning," she said. "I'm getting deployed again." She watched Mark's features closely, hating the flicker of relief that came and went in the blink of an eye.

Turning his head, Mark stared at the picture on the wall opposite the couch. It was a framed photo from their Christmas photoshoot a few months back. "Where are they sending you this time? And for how long?" He took another drink.

Chris studied his profile. At times like this, he barely resembled the man she'd fallen in love with some ten years ago. This version of Mark was tired, or maybe haggard was a better description for the way time had altered him. "You know I can't tell you any of that," she finally said.

"Surprise, surprise."

Chris ignored the bitterness laced through those four syllables. He'd known this was what he was getting into when he married her. The missions, the family…it had all been a part of the package from the very beginning. "I've arranged for my mom to come down tomorrow morning," she said.

"When do you leave?"

"Tomorrow night."

A silent, derisive laugh rocked Mark's chest, and he took another drink. "A whole day to get your shit in order. How generous of them."

Our shit, Chris thought. "I got everything to make chicken enchilada casserole tonight," she said instead. It was his favorite. "I figured we could at least have a nice family dinner before I go…maybe open a bottle of red? So maybe you could cut back on the beer for—"

Mark tilted his beer back, chugging the rest of the can. "Yeah, sure," he said as he lowered it, crunching the empty aluminum in his fist. "Whatever you want, babe." He stood and set the unopened beer on the kitchen counter, then crossed to the hallway that led to the bedrooms. He slammed the door to their bathroom.

Five seconds later, the screen on the baby monitor turned on, sensing motion, and one of the boys started crying.

"You can't tell anyone any of that," Chris said from the passenger seat of Jason's truck. It had been a year since her last deployment, and things were finally going well at home. She pulled up one leg, tucking her bare foot under her thigh and angling herself toward the driver's seat as much as she could without unbuckling her seatbelt. "Seriously, Cartwright." She stared at the side of his face. "If you tell a single person any of what I just told you, I'll beat the shit out of you."

Jason stifled a chuckle, but the humor faded fast. "I'm just glad things have gotten better for you." He shot her a sidelong glance. "You seem happier than you've been in a while. Now I know why."

Chris wasn't sure why she'd decided to spill the beans to Jason on the issues she and Mark had been having over the past four years. It's not like anything about Jason Cartwright and his stony personality screamed, "Share your feelings with me!" He was the typical Green Beret—badass and coldhearted. Chris laughed to herself and shook her head. It was that third whiskey, most likely. Liquor always loosened her tongue.

But things with her and Mark, especially with Mark and the boys, really were better. Almost like night and day from the way they'd been a year ago.

"I'll miss having your smart-ass self around, though," Jason said. They weren't in the same unit—they weren't even in the same branch of the Special Forces. Jason was a Green Beret to Chris's Army Ranger. But their respective units worked together enough that they'd come to know each other well.

Chris smiled, just a little. "That was the deal—my resignation for his drinking." Felt sort of hypocritical now, in her more-than-slightly-buzzed state. But Mark had given Chris the okay to let loose on her girls' night out. Hell, it had been his idea for her to go out in the first place. He'd offered to watch the boys. It was the sweetest thing he'd done for her in a long, *long* time.

"Well, I'm happy for you." Jason brought the truck to a stop, and Chris glanced out her window, surprised to find her driveway and house on the other side of the glass already.

"Thanks," Chris said, straightening in her seat and unbuckling her seatbelt. She reached for the door handle, cracking the door open, then glanced back at Jason. "And thanks for the ride. I think you chauffeuring us home made Carly and Jamie's night."

Jason flashed her a mischievous smile, deepening his dimples. "But not yours."

Chris hopped out of the truck and turned to face Jason. "Yes, Sir—not crashing as I drove my tipsy ass home definitely made my night."

Jason winked. "My best to the wife and kids."

"Shut your mouth, pretty boy," Chris said with a laugh and shut the truck door.

Humming some tuneless song, she walked—mostly in a straight line—up the driveway, turning to veer up the paved path to the front door. When Jason revved his engine, she waved goodbye without looking. He would wait until she got into the house to drive away, even though he knew she could more than take care of herself. He could be a gentleman where ladies were concerned, especially when he wasn't interested in getting into the pants of the lady in question.

Chris was still humming as she made her way into the living room. She could just see the top of Mark's head over the back of the recliner, and based on the infomercial for a combo mop-broom-squeegee playing on the TV, he was fast asleep. He must've tried to stay up, waiting to go to bed until Chris came home, safe and sound, from the big girls' night out.

Once again, Chris found herself smiling, and once again, her happiness was genuine. It felt like such a long time since smiles had come so easily, and now they were all too frequent. The sense of contentment felt strange, but it was also insanely welcome.

Chris's smile wilted when she rounded the recliner to wake her husband. He was passed out, but not from sleep. Not from waiting up for her. Not if the beer can slipping from his limp grasp was anything to go by. A can of beer that hadn't been in the house when she'd left, meaning Mark must've gone out to get it. And he must've gone after the boys were asleep, leaving them alone, because four-year-olds don't do secrets. He'd *left them alone*…

That lying piece of shit—he must've planned this all along.

He'd probably planned on cleaning up the evidence before she got home, only he passed out first.

A cold calm surrounded Chris, chasing away the last remnants of intoxication. Logic became her lifeboat, keeping her afloat amidst a sea of disappointment. Action—no, necessity became the tunnel blocking out the inferno of rage roaring to life within her. That mother fucker—

Chris shook her head. Not now. She couldn't do this right now. Mark had broken the last straw, and she had things to do.

Head held high, she snatched the beer can off the floor and threw it into the recycle bin containing the remnants of an entire twelve-pack, then made her way to the hallway, heading for the boys' room.

She'd threatened to leave before, but now she was beyond threats. Now was the time for follow-through. For consequences. For strength. She could give in to the maelstrom of emotion later. Right this moment, she had to take care of the boys. Of herself.

Tucked into their matching twin beds, the boys slept soundly, one on his back, the other curled up in a ball on his side. She'd give them this night, this one last moment of peace and happiness, before tearing it all away. In the morning, their world would fall apart.

Chris eased the door shut.

And no matter what Mark said, no matter what he made her feel or how he blamed her, this—the destruction of her boys' world—was *not* her fault.

Sleep wasn't even the remotest of options, so Chris spent the evening sobering up and making plans and packing. There was only one person who knew about the troubles she and her husband had been having. Sure, her mom suspected, but Chris wasn't ready to face her and the myriad of questions and pitying looks she was guaranteed to smother Chris with as soon as her motherly suspicions were confirmed, however well intended.

Morning came as always, the rising sun illuminating an unwavering sense of resolve within Chris. She was done with Mark's false promises—with his lies—and she felt stronger than she had in a long time. She'd already started untangling the emotional knots tying her to her husband. Maybe in a few years...maybe if he could get sober and prove that he could make it—that he *wanted* to make it—she'd consider reuniting with him. But not a day sooner. Not when he'd endangered their boys with his negligence. She wouldn't give an inch on this.

Mark never came to bed, which was a relief. If he had, Chris thought she might've been so repulsed that she'd have gone and slept on the couch. Then he would've known something was up. That would only have made things harder.

She was lying on her side, her back to the bedroom door, when he finally trudged into their room. She listened as the shower ran, as he gagged while brushing his teeth—he always did that after a bender—and as he dressed near the foot of the bed.

He sat on the edge of the mattress for a few minutes, and the hairs on the back of Chris's neck stood on end. Was he looking at her? Watching her? What was he feeling? Regret? Shame? Or did he feel relief, thinking he'd gotten away with it?

Somehow, Chris managed to convince herself that she didn't care.

Finally, Mark stood and left for work. Chris waited until she heard the hum of the garage door shutting. She waited for five more minutes, then another five, just to make sure Mark wasn't returning. She wanted to leave while he was at work, cowardly as it felt. If everything went according to plan, any confrontation between Chris and Mark would happen out of earshot of the boys. That's what was best for them, which was all that mattered now.

She was fully dressed under the covers, and her bags were packed and stowed in her car already. All she had to do was pack the boys' things, a week or two's worth of clothes, and enough toys to hold them over until she could figure out a more permanent situation. She just hoped her resolve could hold over until then, too.

The morning passed in a rush. Chris recognized the symptoms of mild shock. She felt disconnected from the world. Numb. Her mind was attempting to protect her from the emotional trauma, holding the brunt of the emotions at bay until she'd had a chance to cool off. Until she wasn't so raw. Until she could deal with her emotions without freaking the boys out as well.

"Are we going to the zoo?" Alex asked from the back seat as Chris pulled her car out of the garage. She'd told the boys they were going on an adventure. The last time she told them that, they'd spent the afternoon at the local petting zoo. Mark had been there, too.

Chris let out a hollow laugh, warming it with her good intentions. "No, baby, this is a brand-new kind of adventure."

Alex beamed at her in the rearview mirror, eyes bright with excitement, with trust. Chris jutted her jaw forward, her own eyes stinging. She would not cry until she could do it behind a closed door. She *would not.*

Jason was expecting them. He'd already made up his guest room for the three of them, and he'd promised they could stay for as long as they needed. His unit would be shipping out on a mission in a few days anyway, he'd told her, so it would be nice to have someone around to watch his house. At least, that's what he claimed when Chris called him in the early hours of the morning.

Jason and the boys were out in the backyard, in the middle of a chaotic game of croquet, when Mark finally showed up that evening. Chris had left a note on the fridge letting Mark know where she and the boys were and why, which Mark had to have seen as soon as he got home from the hospital that afternoon. Based on his bleary eyes, his wobbly state, and the pungent scent of alcohol wafting off him, he'd self-medicated his wounded feelings with the better part of a bottle of vodka before heading over to confront Chris.

She'd been watching for him out the front window while Jason kept the boys entertained. She'd known he would show up eventually; she just hadn't guessed he'd be that far gone by the time he did.

"Come on, baby," Mark said, shoulders drooped and voice pleading. He stood on the stoop, the screen door the only thing separating him from Chris. "Come home. Bring the boys. Please… I need you. I—" He bowed his head, his shoulders shaking. He said something more, but the words were incoherent, muddled by the drink and his sobs.

"Go home, Mark," Chris said. "We'll talk tomorrow, when you've sobered up."

Mark sniffled and raised his head. "But—" Whatever he'd been about to say, whatever pleas he'd planned to utter, Chris never found out. His focus drifted past her and he straightened, swaying a bit, his chest puffing out.

Chris let out a sigh and glanced over her shoulder. Sure enough, Jason stood there, arms crossed over his broad chest and his face set in a hard scowl.

"So that's what this is about?" Mark slurred. "I knew there was something going on. How long have you been fucking this—"

"I have never cheated on you, Mark," Chris said, calm and composed on the surface but raging within. "You need to leave, now." She didn't want the boys to overhear them, especially not when Mark was like this. "We'll talk tomorrow."

He sneered. "Where're the boys?" He leaned in, placing his palms on the screen, and craned his neck to see around Chris. "Boys!" he called. "Come on, Daddy's going to take you home."

Chris's eyes widened, and she looked back at Jason once more. No words were needed; he nodded once, then retreated further into the house to keep the boys distracted.

Once Jason was out of sight, Chris refocused on her miserable, piece-of-shit husband. "You are not driving our children *anywhere*. Get out of here," she said, gritting her teeth. "Now, Mark, or I swear to God, I will call the police and have them drag you away for trespassing." The boys would not see him like this. They would *not*.

Mark backed up a few steps, stumbling when he reached the porch stairs. "Whore," he said and spat on the porch before starting down the walkway. Chris resisted the bait and remained silent.

Mark stopped after a few uneven strides and turned back to the house, raising a hand to point at Chris. "I'll fight you for the boys. I'll tell the judge whatever he wants to hear to keep them from you. You're an *unfit mother*."

Fear clutched Chris's heart, and despite her resolve to be silent, she couldn't stop the words from pouring out. "You act like you care!" she shouted back. "You don't want them—you've *never* wanted them."

A callous, knowing smile parted Mark's lips as if he'd stumbled across gold. "I'll fight with everything I've got."

"Go ahead and try."

"Don't think I won't," Mark said, resuming his wobbly way back to his car.

"You will never take them," she vowed, her hands clenching to fists.

Chris watched him fumble with the lock on the sedan. She curled her lip when, after a good thirty seconds, he discovered that the door was already unlocked. She didn't feel even an ounce of responsibility as she watched him drive away. Some twisted, desperate part of her hoped he'd crash. Then maybe this would all finally be over with.

She heard Jason's quiet footsteps before he rested his hand on her shoulder. He didn't say anything. No "Are you alright?" No "It'll get better." He was just there, which was exactly what Chris needed.

"I wish I'd never met him," she said, voice barely audible.

"That's not true," Jason said. "Then you wouldn't have the boys."

Chris's shoulders slumped, and her head drooped. The weight

of everything she was losing—of everything she might lose—threatened to push her through the floor. To bury her. She was one of the first women to become an Army Ranger. She'd survived sieges and guerilla warfare. But losing the boys…she wasn't sure she could survive that.

Raising her head, Chris glared at the place where Mark's car had been just moments ago. "Then I wish he'd just die."

Jason gave her shoulder a squeeze. But he didn't refute her statement, not this time.

Because he knew, in that moment, she spoke the truth.

7

JULY 7, 2 AE

With all that goes on here at the farm, it's easy to forget the little things that keep us going. We're so busy all the time; even our family dinners seem trumped more often than not by something someone has to do before sunset, or someone has to take off on another trip of some sort. So, I got to thinking...

With the help and contributions of everyone on the farm, I'm going to start a survival handbook, one we can distribute to new colonists throughout the local outposts to use as their guides instead of having us teach them everything. I figure it's a way to slow our lives down so we might be able to enjoy our good fortunes again and bask in the sunshine, like I did today with Dani and baby Ceara up on the hill, under the tree. We were having an impromptu girls' retreat, and we got to talking about our teenage years and how there hadn't been much more than boys and college on our minds. Dani mentioned our road trip up the coast, and we realized that was the summer that changed everything for us. We grew up. She moved away. Yet, somehow, here we are, still chugging along and doing it together.

While this memory may not be as monumental as some of the

others, it's important to me. It reminds me of "Dani and Zoe"—unaltered and naïve. It reminds me of everything we've been through together, the good and the bad and the crazy and the fun. Anyway, important or not, seeing as this is my journal, I'll record whatever I'd like.

"D, don't you think we should pull over and check the—"

Dani tossed Zoe a sidelong glance. "It's just hot out, Zo. I'm sure the engine's fine." Despite her assurances, Dani eyed the temperature dial on her new-old Mini Cooper's dashboard. The needle was precariously close to the red "danger zone." Close, but not quite there.

She took a deep breath, straightening her back as she exhaled and flashing Zoe her trademark brilliant smile. The engine couldn't overheat. Not on this trip. It was a last-hurrah trip—even if Dani had yet to divulge that little snippet to Zoe—and the universe wouldn't let something like a faulty radiator destroy such a sacred thing. *Dani* wouldn't allow it, dammit. She *wouldn't.*

Zoe rolled down her window and stuck her hand outside, then turned to stare at Dani, who purposely ignored her best friend's pointed look. "It's maybe seventy-five degrees out there, D. I don't think the air temperature is the problem."

Eyes stinging with the threat of tears, Dani blinked several times, then cleared her throat. This trip was supposed to be perfect. Their "we survived graduation" road trip. Their last carefree adventure before Dani ruined everything with six dreaded words—*I'm going to school in Washington.*

There was nothing but winding road ahead and behind, and the Pacific Ocean cuddled up to them to the left. They'd spent the previous night camping surrounded by towering redwoods, and the morning and early afternoon had been filled with the two eighteen-year-olds singing along to CD after CD loaded up with all their favorite songs. So far, the trip *was* perfect. Except for the part where Dani hadn't worked up the nerve to confess her future plans to Zoe.

Dani breathed in, intending to offer up more deflections about the car's ever-rising temperature, and promptly wrinkled her nose. The interior of the car suddenly stunk like burnt maple syrup.

"Oh, shit—that is definitely not normal," Zoe said. "Seriously, D, it's time to pull over."

Eyes watering, both from the influx of smoke billowing in through the vents and from the suspicion that the trip was about to come to an abrupt, early end, Dani pulled onto the shoulder and shut the engine off, the smoke dispersing soon after. Dani and Zoe flung their doors open, fanning the smoke that remained within the car's interior and taking deep breaths.

"Oh, come on," Zoe groaned, staring down at her cell phone. She speared Dani with her brilliant teal eyes. "No signal." Squinting, Zoe peered around at the landscape surrounding them off the shoulder. "Being up high is supposed to help, right? I'm going to climb up there," she said, pointing to the steep hillside. She hastily climbed out of the car and peered in through the open door at Dani. "You should get out, take a deep breath. That smoke is probably toxic."

Dani shrugged, avoiding Zoe's gaze. If she looked at her, really looked at her, she'd start crying. Tears were her body's go-to response with pretty much any strong emotion, be it anger, frustration, disappointment, or, appropriately, sadness. At the moment, she was fending off an avalanche of all of those, and more.

"Hey…" Zoe leaned farther into the car and gave Dani's arm a squeeze. "We'll figure this out. We always do."

Dani sniffled and looked away. But she nodded, too.

"Be right back," Zoe said, then shut the door.

Dani rested her forehead on the top of the steering wheel, turning her head to watch Zoe scale the steep hill. The bottom half of her legs were lost in the tall grasses covering the hillside, and as she crested the hill, the rest of her gradually disappeared as well.

Dani held her breath.

A few seconds later, Zoe reappeared, scowling and giving Dani a thumbs-down. No luck, then.

Dani blew out the breath she'd been holding in a quiet, bitter laugh. She was starting to think this whole trip was cursed. Or maybe it was just karma for withholding the truth from Zoe for so long. For two months. She'd made the decision to go to college out of state *two whole months* ago but hadn't had the nerve to admit it to Zoe. For the first few weeks, she hadn't even been able to admit it to herself.

Zoe carefully made her way back down the hillside, skidding and stumbling a time or two. When she reached the gravelly turnout, she leaned her forearms on the frame of the open passenger side window and poked her head into the car. "Come on, D," she said, giving a sideways nod toward the back of the car. "Let's stand out here and look damselly. Some guy's bound to stop to help."

Dani straightened and twisted in her seat to look out the rear windshield. She drew one side of her bottom lip between her teeth, perking up a bit. This mission was right up her alley; if there was one thing she could do well, it was look helpless. Unlike Zoe, who was tall and curvy and walked with definite purpose—her confidence left no doubt that she'd be able to accomplish whatever she set her mind to—Dani was cute and petite, verging on childlike. She made up for it with her spitfire personality, but that didn't always help matters. Usually her diminutive size annoyed her, but now—for once—it might actually prove useful.

Dani pushed the car door open and slipped out, rubbing her hands together. Now that she had a task—get somebody to stop and help them—she was feeling less despondent. "Should we show some skin?" she asked, wiggling her eyebrows at Zoe over the roof of the car. Another vehicle had yet to pass them, and she didn't want to risk losing a potential rescuer. This trip could still be salvaged; if they got the car to a shop and the repairs could be made with little time or expense, they'd be able to continue on their way, no harm done.

Zoe snorted, giving Dani elevator eyes as she rounded the rear bumper. "*More* skin?"

Dani glanced down at herself. Cutoff jean shorts and a tank top didn't leave much in the way of options for her—she was already showing about as much skin as was legal in public. But Zoe was wearing jeans and a t-shirt, and she was the one with all the curves, after all.

"By *we*, I was actually referring to *you*," Dani said, giving Zoe's chest a pointed look. "You're the one with the goods."

Zoe raised a single eyebrow.

"Maybe just knot up the bottom of your shirt?" Dani suggested, leaning her hip against the back of the car and holding in a giggle. Zoe's flat stare was just so Zoe. Dani couldn't resist egging her on. She reached for the hem of Zoe's t-shirt. "Show off your six-pack?"

Zoe slapped Dani's hand away, laughing through her nose. "Six-pack," she muttered. "More like one-pack."

Dani let her giggle fly free.

"I'm sure we'll manage without resorting to—"

At the sound of an engine, both girls turned their heads to watch the winding stretch of highway behind them. Dani stepped closer to the road, and with a few quick footsteps, Zoe joined her.

The truck was hidden by the hillside, coming into view as it barreled around a curve in the road. It was an older pickup, something from the eighties, painted a ridiculous neon green and raised up on monstrous tires. Four guys were piled in, two in the cab and two lounging in the truck bed.

Dani shrank back a step at the sight of them and the sound of their raucous, hooting laughter. Zoe, however, held her ground.

“Zo,” Dani said, reaching out and gripping Zoe’s elbow. She shook her head ever so slightly.

Zoe glanced over her shoulder at Dani, flashing her a tight but reassuring smile.

The truck slowed, coming to a stop on the road beside Dani’s car. “Hellooo, ladies,” the guy in the passenger seat said, grin lecherous and gaze greedy. He looked like he was a few years older than them. “You seem to be in some trouble, and we’re more than willing to give you a hand.”

“Yeah we are,” one of the guys from the back of the truck shouted, cajoling his buddy.

Zoe took a single step closer to the truck. “We just need a ride into the next town.” She stood a little straighter, squaring her shoulders. Dani doubted she even knew she was doing it. “But it looks like you’re overloaded as it is,” Zoe added, pointing to the back of the truck with her chin. “We’ll wait for someone else.”

“Aw…there’s plenty of room,” the guy in the passenger seat said. He licked his lips and glanced at the driver, sly grin curving his lips. “We, ah, just need a little compensation.”

Dani narrowed her eyes.

“How much?” Zoe asked.

The passenger’s eyes veered lower on Zoe’s body, then returned to her face. “How about you lift up your shirt, there, and we’ll call it even. How’s that sound?” His buddies in the back of the truck guffawed, but the driver at least looked a little uncomfortable.

Dani glared. Couldn’t say she hadn’t seen that one coming, but it was still a bit of a shock to her ears.

Zoe was quiet for a moment, so long that Dani thought she might actually be considering the trade. “How about you go fuck yourself—how’s that sound?”

The passenger’s expression darkened. “Let these bitches walk,” he said, looking to the driver. Not two seconds later, the truck was driving away.

"Assholes," Zoe said, turning and stomping back toward Dani.

"Maybe we *should* just walk." Dani brushed a flyaway tendril of fiery red hair from her face. "That last sign said the next town was only five miles away. We can manage that."

"Yeah," Zoe said, combing her fingers through her long, dark hair and tying it back in a ponytail using the hair tie stored on her wrist. "That might be our best option." She sent a pointed look down at Dani's feet. "You want to change your shoes first?"

"Pfft," Dani said, waving Zoe's question away with her hand. "Flip-flops are the new tennis shoes."

Zoe let out a dry laugh and made her way to the passenger side of the car to retrieve her messenger bag. "Fine, but if you get blisters, I don't want to hear about it."

Dani rolled her eyes. "Deal."

Two minutes into their stroll, another car approached, this time coming from the opposite direction. It didn't slow, but that wasn't surprising, considering it had yet to pass Dani's smokestack of a car. To the driver, Dani and Zoe were just two young women out for a stroll.

Several more cars passed, coming from both directions, but none stopped. The next car to slow came from the same way the girls had, but it didn't stop. It was a silver sedan, early nineties, the paint oxidized at the edges. Only two guys this time. They slowed to a crawl until they were keeping pace with Dani and Zoe.

"Damn…" The single word was drawn out, a sign of appreciation that came across as nothing but creepy.

Dani watched them out of the corner of her eye, but Zoe kept her gaze straight ahead.

"You girls looking for a good time?"

Without even glancing at them, Zoe raised her left hand, middle finger standing tall.

The guys laughed, and without another word, they sped away.

The next car to pass coming from the road behind them slowed as well. "That your car back there on the side of the road?" the driver asked through the open passenger side window of his pickup.

"We're good, thanks," Zoe said, eyes on the way ahead.

Dani glanced at the guy. His truck was newer, its dark gray paint shimmering in the sunlight. The driver was a little scruffy looking with his slightly too-long hair and nine-o'clock shadow, but his eyes held none of the malice she'd seen from the others.

Like the previous car, the truck inched along beside Dani and Zoe. "If you need a lift into—"

"I said we're fine," Zoe snapped, waving him on. "Keep on driving."

Dani watched the guy's reaction out of the corner of her eye. His eyebrows lifted, his mouth tensing. "I only ask because—"

"Dude," Zoe said. "Seriously. We don't need your help. Just go."

The guy shook his head. "Have it your way." His focus shifted to Dani's face. "Enjoy the walk," he said with a nod, then rolled up his window and drove off.

"He didn't seem so bad," Dani said, watching the back of his truck.

Zoe set her jaw.

"Did you even look at him?" Dani elbowed Zoe's arm. "He was pretty studly." When Zoe gave her the raised-eyebrow look that said *Really?* with more sarcasm than words ever could, Dani grinned. "He had that whole mysterious, broody vibe going for him, too. Pure Zoe bait…"

"Zoe's not hungry right now."

Dani laughed. "Zoe needs to stop talking about herself in the third person." Smirking, she linked her arm with Zoe's and added, "And Dani knows that Zoe's always hungry for dessert."

"I'm really sorry, ma'am, but we don't do European makes," the guy from Chuck's Auto Shop said over the phone. "Just American and Japanese here." His voice went beyond gravelly, like he'd smoked a pack a day since kindergarten and usually followed that up with a pint of whiskey.

Dani fiddled with the pay phone's cord and chewed on her lip, studiously avoiding Zoe's questioning stare. Not that it did any good; Dani was sure Zoe could read the bad news all over her face, anyway.

"But the Autoworks should be able to handle your Mini Cooper," the guy on the phone said.

Dani felt her whole self brighten with the news. "Really?" She met Zoe's eyes, lips spreading into a hopeful smile.

"Yes, ma'am. Now, I know I got their number around here somewhere…"

Dani snapped her fingers a couple times. "Pen," she mouthed to Zoe.

Zoe nodded once, then bent her neck as she dug through her messenger bag. It only took her a few seconds to find a pen; not surprising, considering she always had at least a dozen drawing implements on her at all times.

"Ah, right…there it is." The guy on the phone cleared his throat. "Winchester Autoworks," he said, then recited a phone number, which Dani jotted down on her wrist. "You tell 'em Harry from Chuck's sent you their way. That should get Gavin off my back." That last was quieter, like he hadn't intended for it to make the journey across the phone line to Dani's ears.

"Will do," Dani said. "Thank you!" She hung up, and before she could even consider searching through the change pooled at the bottom of her shoulder bag, Zoe handed her the quarter and dime she needed to make another phone call. "Thanks," she said, flashing her best friend a smile before feeding the coins into the slot and dialing the number written in ink on her wrist.

The phone rang four times before someone answered. "Winchester Automotive," a woman said, laughter in her voice. "Stop," she whispered to someone, then cleared her throat. "This is Agatha. How can I help you?"

The corner of Dani's mouth lifted. "Hi, I'm Dani. Um…Harry from Chuck's gave me your number."

"He did, did he?"

"Uh-huh," Dani said with a slight nod. "You see…" She explained the situation with her car and its current abandoned, overheated state.

"And where are you now, Dani?" Agatha asked.

Dani turned, eyes searching for the gas station's sign. "The Shell station at the—" She paused, taking a millisecond to orient herself to the cardinal directions. "The south end of town."

"Alrighty," Agatha said, tone chipper. "We'll have a tow truck there to pick you up in ten minutes. Once we get you and your car back here, we'll give it a quick look over and be able to give you an estimate."

"Awesome," Dani said, relief heavy in her voice. She remained ever hopeful that the damage would be quick, easy, and cheap to fix. This trip *would* be salvaged, damn it.

Dani sat squished against the tow truck's passenger door. She was sharing the seat with Zoe, who'd refused to remain at the gas station when the truck showed up with only a single seat to spare. Dani stared out the window, absently chewing on her thumbnail as she considered the best way to fess up the truth to Zoe. Sooner was certainly better than later. The only problem with sooner was that it was, well, *sooner*.

"You gals sure are lucky," Billy, the tow truck driver, said. He was a rough-and-tumble middle-aged man whose hands were so callused it was impressive that he could still curl his fingers around the steering wheel.

Dani certainly didn't feel lucky—in fact, it *felt* like Lady Luck was punking her—though she didn't say so out loud.

"Why's that?" Zoe asked.

Dani tore her gaze from the sprawling view of the ocean beyond the window to look at Billy.

"It's been a slow day, and Aggy was just fixing to close up shop," he said. "Had you gals called ten minutes later, you would've had to wait until tomorrow to find out the damage."

Zoe turned her face to Dani and the two exchanged a look—eyebrows raised, lips curved into tight, close-lipped smiles.

"Aggy'll be gone by the time you get to the shop—she just helps out when the shop's short-staffed—but Gavin'll be there to look over your car, and Aggy left the paperwork out for him to go over with you, so there shouldn't be any holdups," Billy said with hardly a break for air. "You girls ever been to Winchester Cove before?"

"No," Zoe said, exchanging another look with Dani. Her vibrant eyes danced with mirth, and Dani had to suppress a giggle. "We're on a road trip. We just graduated."

"Did you now?" Billy said. "Whereabouts are you girls from?"

"Bodega Bay," Zoe told him.

Billy raised his eyebrows. "Whereabouts is that?"

"California," Zoe said. "On the coast, just a little ways north of San Francisco."

"Ah…beautiful country. And what's next for you girls? College? Work?" Billy slowed the tow truck as they pulled into town. "Or are you two going to take one of those gap years I keep hearing about?"

Dani's stomach knotted up. This was not the place she wanted to have this conversation with Zoe, scrunched in the passenger seat of a tow truck and with an audience. Her pulse raced, and she licked her lips, thoughts stalled by fear.

Luckily, Billy continued rambling, carrying on the conversation on his own. "My nephew took one of them, and he's been in

Australia for the past two years. My sister's starting to worry he might never come home." He slowed the truck to a crawl and turned left into a gravel lot. Through the windshield, Dani could see the sign for Winchester Autoworks. "And here we are."

Dani exhaled in relief. Not wanting the conversation to revert to the topic of college once more, even for a second, she pointed to the single open garage door ahead. "Do we go in there?"

"Yes, ma'am," Billy said, opening his door. "Just you follow me. I'll introduce you to Gavin, then come back here to let your car down."

The gravel crunched under their shoes, Dani's flip-flops smacking against the bottoms of her feet, as they approached the shop, Billy in the lead and Dani and Zoe following close behind him. Dani paused for a moment when the mechanic stepped into view, hardly able to believe her eyes.

Dani reached for Zoe's wrist, giving it a squeeze. She leaned in and whispered, "That's the guy from earlier—the Zoe bait."

Zoe quirked one eyebrow, interest dancing in her teal stare and color rising in her cheeks.

"Gavin," Billy said when they reached the shop, "this is Dani" —he pointed to Dani with his thumb—"and Zoe," he added, pointing to her in turn. "Dani's the owner of the car," he said matter-of-factly, then turned and, gravel crunching under his work boots, made his way back to the tow truck.

"Glad you finally made it," Gavin said, hazel eyes alight with amusement.

Dani glanced at Zoe, whose blush had deepened in embarrassment, then stepped forward. "Nice to meet you...officially," Dani said, sticking out her hand. Gavin shook it gently, his hand engulfing hers, and gave a slight nod. "And sorry about earlier. We'd had a couple bad encounters already, so..."

"Figured as much," Gavin said, crossing his arms over his chest and leaning back against the trunk of a shiny black classic muscle car Dani wouldn't have been able to name had her life depended on it. “Why don’t you head into the office.” He pointed further into the shop with his chin to where an interior window displayed two desks laden with paperwork, a half-dozen chairs, a water cooler, and a small table with a coffeepot, a bowl of apples and bananas, and a pastel pink bakery box. “Aggy made a fresh pot of coffee just before she left, and I’m pretty sure there’s still a couple donuts left in the box.”

Dani was already salivating, and Zoe let out an almost inaudible groan. Dani had a sweet tooth a mile long, and Zoe was a straight-up coffee addict; had been ever since she started working afternoons at the café sophomore year.

“Thank you,” Dani said to Gavin before following Zoe, who was already lured deeper into the shop by the promise of coffee. “Is there anything I should read over or sign while we wait in there?” she asked over her shoulder.

Gavin shook his head. “I’ll go over it all with you once I’ve had a look at your car.”

Dani gave him a thumbs-up, then picked up the pace, trotting to catch up with Zoe. She needed sugar. And caffeine. And, above all else, a spine.

The little office was homey—much more so than she’d expected of an auto shop. The desks were cluttered but organized, the cushioned chairs in the waiting area were simple but comfortable, and the whole room smelled of coffee and vanilla air freshener. And there were, in fact, a few donuts left in that beautiful pink baker’s box.

“A maple bar!” Dani exclaimed with glee. She glanced at Zoe, who was doctoring a cup of coffee. “Do you mind if I take it?” She knew that Zoe liked maple bars, too, though maybe not quite as fanatically as Dani did.

Zoe tossed her stir stick into the little trashcan on the floor under the table and looked at Dani. “I can’t believe you’re even asking me that. When have I ever come between you and a maple bar?”

Dani gave her a sheepish smile. "Well, I didn't want to be rude and hog the best donut."

Zoe snorted a laugh. "Since when?"

Slowly, Dani shrugged. The guilt caused by withholding her college plans from Zoe made her feel like a dirtbag.

"Take the damn donut, D," Zoe said, waving to the open box. "I'm in more of a sprinkles mood, anyway." She raised her disposable coffee cup to her lips and took a sip, closing her eyes and moaning softly.

Dani picked up the maple bar. "Thinking about Gavin?"

Zoe coughed, her eyes popping open. "Shit," she hissed as hot coffee splashed out of the cup and over her hand.

Dani took a bite of her donut, chest convulsing with silent laughter as she chewed. "You were," she said, watching Zoe wipe off her hand with a wad of paper napkins. "You were thinking about him. I knew it!"

Primly, Zoe retrieved her coffee cup from the table and reached into the donut box, plucking out the cake donut with white frosting and multicolored sprinkles. She brought the donut up to her mouth, her lips quirking into a sly grin. "Maybe," she said, then took a bite.

Dani giggled. "Hot name, too, right?" She set her donut down on a napkin and started fixing her own cup of coffee. "Gaaavinnn," she said, drawing the name out luxuriously.

"Mm-hmm," Zoe said as she sat in one of the chairs. She set her donut on a napkin on the end table, wrapping both hands around her coffee cup. "How old do you think he is?"

Dani eyed Zoe over her shoulder. *About as old as Jason* was her first thought; not that it was a surprising thought, considering she measured every guy against her forever crush, a.k.a. Zoe's older brother, who was four years their senior. "Mid to late twenties, maybe?" she said, then narrowed her eyes when she processed Zoe's considering expression. "You're seriously considering flirting with him, aren't you?"

Zoe shrugged at first, then looked at Dani and winked, a sly smile curving her lips. "Depends on how long we're here."

"Three days?" Dani said, eyes bugging out.

Standing behind the nearest of the two desks, Gavin nodded. "Because of the weekend. The parts should come on Monday." He squinted, tilting his head to the side. "Maybe Tuesday. Once they're here, it'll only take me a couple hours to do the repair, and then you can be on your way."

Dani stood, leaving Zoe to guard their little coffee-and-donut stash, and approached the desk. "And there's no way to do, like, a rush delivery or something?"

"Well, yeah," Gavin said, "but it'll cost you more than the repair itself." Which wouldn't matter so much, except funds were limited.

Dani let her head fall back and groaned. She could hear Zoe's soft footfalls approach from behind her.

Zoe hooked her arm with Dani's. "So it looks like we'll be here for a few nights," she said.

Pouting her lower lip, Dani rested her head on Zoe's shoulder.

"Do you have any recommendations for where to stay?" After a brief pause, Zoe added, "And what to do with all of our free time while we're here?" Dani wasn't sure if Gavin could pick up on the veiled invitation in Zoe's question, but she sure as hell could. Based on his genuinely thoughtful expression, not so much.

"There's a bed-and-breakfast out on the bluff—used to be an old lighthouse. Folks seem to like staying there."

Dani frowned, thinking it sounded expensive.

"Anything closer to town?" Zoe asked.

"Maybe a motel…or a campground?" Dani added.

Gavin nodded slowly. "There's the Super 8 just up the road, and the Winchester Inn at the north edge of town." He laughed gruffly. "And don't let the name fool you—they're taking great liberties by using the word 'inn' in their name. I'd go for the Super 8…to avoid the hourly crowd, if you catch my drift."

Dani choked on nothing but saliva and air. "You mean *prostitutes*?"

Zoe squeezed her elbow. "Thanks for the tip."

With a slight nod, Gavin continued, "And as for camping, there's a KOA near the bluff. Nice spot—beach access and views of the ocean—but it's maybe a half a mile away from town. Not quite as far as the B and B, but not exactly in town, either."

"That sounds nice," Dani said, looking at Zoe. They had all the gear for it; camping had been their plan for most of their stops, anyway, with a few motels mixed in for the sole purpose of having access to a long, hot shower.

"It does," Zoe said absently. Dani could practically see the gears turning inside Zoe's head. "Gavin," Zoe said, "I don't suppose you'd be able to give us a ride to the campground? It's just that it'll be kind of a trek for us, carrying all of our stuff and all…" And then he'd know exactly where to find them, should his thoughts fixate on Zoe as much as hers were fixated on him.

Dani had to turn away to hide her grin.

"Shouldn't be a problem."

"What do you want to do for dinner?" Dani asked Zoe over the tiny whirr of the motor inflating the air mattress. On the short drive out to the campground, Gavin had given them a quick tour of the town—not that there was much of it. Their food options were limited to a café, a pizza joint, a bar and grill, and a straight-up pub.

"Let's go to the Pour House," Zoe said, referring to the pub. "Put those fake IDs to good use."

"Mmmm…" Dani closed her eyes and smacked her lips. "Fish and chips sounds delish."

"And a pint of beer," Zoe added.

Dani made an *ick* face. "Do you think they'll have wine coolers?"

Zoe threw her pillow at Dani. "If you order a wine cooler, I'll make fun of you for it for the rest of our lives."

Dani tossed the pillow right back at Zoe. "Puh-*lease*," she laughed. "You like them just as much as I do."

"I do not," Zoe said, swatting the pillow away.

Dani raised her eyebrows and cocked her head to the side.

"Fine," Zoe admitted, rolling her eyes. "I like them. But I also like beer."

"Do not."

Zoe settled a level stare at Dani, and Dani mimicked her. "Fine," Zoe said. "I don't like it; it tastes like piss." She raised a finger. "But I'm determined to learn to appreciate it."

Laughing, Dani shook her head. She took a deep breath and scanned the interior of their cavernous tent. This was only the third time they'd set it up since leaving Bodega Bay, but they'd already settled into an easy routine. "I think we're good to go. Should we head into town…get started on your beer appreciation quest?"

"Yeah," Zoe said. "Just one sec." She pulled her t-shirt off over her head, swapping it for a black blousier shirt with a deep V-neck. "What do you think?" she asked Dani as she adjusted the neckline to show an ample amount of cleavage.

"Yowza," Dani said, wiggling her eyebrows.

"Too much? I don't want to be confused with those *hourly* patrons at the motel, but we might need the extra incentive to get into the bar."

Dani shook her head. "It's just enough."

"Alright." Zoe rubbed her hands together eagerly. "Let's get this show on the road."

The walk back to town was uneventful, and within ten minutes, they were settling in at the Pour House at a high table near the bar. The place was packed, but then, it was Friday night, and this seemed to be the only bar in town.

"What if the IDs don't work?" Dani asked, clutching her little purse on her lap. It was her first time in a twenty-one-and-over establishment, and she felt certain she would get kicked out at any second.

Unconcerned, Zoe went about arranging her jean jacket on the back of her chair, then combed her fingers through her hair, pulling it up into a ponytail. "We'll be fine, D. Trust me."

And, as usual, Zoe was right. The server scrutinized their IDs, especially Dani's, but handed them back without complaint. "So that was a cider and a Hefeweizen?" she said, pointing to Dani and Zoe in turn.

Dani nodded. "And can I get the fish and chips? Extra tartar sauce?"

"You got it."

While the server took Zoe's food order, Dani scanned the people in the packed bar, keeping an eye out for Gavin. Though, if he were there, she was certain Zoe would've noticed already.

Not a stool was empty at the bar proper. Most were filled by men, though there was one couple at the corner, and a pair of middle-aged women was seated at the shorter stretch of bar. They were the most raucous of the bunch, laughing joyously as they sipped their cocktails and whispered to one another, not a care in the world.

"I'll be right out with your drinks," the server said.

"Thanks," Zoe said, and Dani flashed the server a quick smile.

"Think that'll be us one day?" Dani asked, a quick flick of her finger singling out that lone pair of women seated at the bar.

"It better be."

The server returned, setting down their drinks and a basket of homemade potato chips. "The kitchen's a little backed up, so it'll take a while for your food. Chips are on the house. And the guy over there at the bar"—she nodded toward the corner with the couple—"would like to buy your drinks."

Dani perked up in her chair, eyes searching for their admirer. "Really?"

Zoe twisted around, doing the same. A second later, her expression soured. "Thanks," she told the server, "but we'll get them ourselves."

Dani leaned forward, elbows on the table. "But Zo…" Dani had never had a guy offer to buy her a drink before. It felt so grown up and somehow classy.

Zoe gave a small shake of her head. "Look who it is, D." She returned her attention to the server. "Really, we're good."

The corner of the server's mouth rose, and she winked. "Good call." She turned and headed back to the bar, finally giving Dani a view of their would-be beverage patron. It was the douchebag who'd been riding in the passenger seat of the wannabe monster truck.

Dani's eyes met his for a fraction of a second, and she hastily looked away, cheeks heating.

"We don't want anything from that dickhead," Zoe said, eyes ablaze.

"At least his friends aren't with him," Dani noted. "He's got nobody to show off for."

Zoe's focus slipped past Dani, her eyes narrowing. "You've got to be kidding me." She looked at Dani. "You just had to say that, didn't you?"

"What?" Dani turned around in her chair, fingers gripping the top rail. Her eyes widened when she spotted the three guys who'd just come in from outside, and she snapped back around to face Zoe. "Oh my God!" She clapped her hands over her mouth. "Sorry!" she mumbled.

Zoe waved the apology away. "Whatever. They can only bother us if we let them." She raised her pint glass. "To us. Whatever else happens in our lives, we'll never lose sight of our true goal."

Dani lifted her own pint glass, raising her eyebrows in question.

Zoe leaned in. "To be *them* one day—happy, laughing, and together," she said, smirking as she glanced at the pair of women sitting at the bar.

Dani grinned and clinked her glass against Zoe's. "To us being them one day," she said and took a drink. The cider was crisp and refreshing, the potato chips were just this side of not too salty and still warm from the fryer, and the atmosphere was ripe with good humor. By the time their food came, Dani had forgotten all about the jerks from earlier…until Zoe muttered a curse.

She set her fresh pint of beer on the table. "We've got incoming."

Dani glanced around, fry in hand. Her stomach did a sickly flip-flop when she spotted two of the guys from the truck approaching—the passenger and one of the jokers from the back. She dropped her fry and fidgeted with the paper napkin as they drew closer, twisting it into knots under the table.

As Zoe had predicted, the guys headed straight for their table. "Ladies," the passenger said, consonants slurring together just a little. "So nice to see you again." He grinned wolfishly. The other stared at Dani, thumb running across his bottom lip.

Dani looked to Zoe, tongue paralyzed. She could flirt her way up one side of this bar and down the other if she wanted, but fending off unwanted attention from douchebags was way out of her wheelhouse. They just never seemed to take her seriously when she said no.

"Can't say the feeling's mutual," Zoe said, voice dry and stare hard.

The passenger held up his hands as though he were surrendering. "Alright, alright, that's fair. I was a dick earlier, I'll admit it."

Dani looked up at him, surprised by the admission. However, he lost whatever ground he might've gained when she saw how obviously his stare kept dropping to Zoe's chest. Sneering, she looked away.

"You staying in town tonight?"

"Why?" Zoe asked, clearly disinterested.

"Maybe we could visit you," he said. "Hang out. Make amends. We're very, very sorry."

"Thanks, but no."

"What? You got something better to do?"

"Yeah," Zoe said, stare flat, voice deadpan.

"What? Each other?" The passenger's expression remained serious, but his buddy giggled, gaze drifting to Zoe but returning to Dani soon enough.

Zoe's only response was an icy glare.

The passenger shrugged. "So I'm right? You're dykes?" He tucked in his chin, that hungry, wolfish grin reemerging. "A couple of scissor sisters." He licked his lips. "God, that's so fucking hot."

"You can leave now," Zoe said, voice hard, glare harder.

"You heard her, Shane," a familiar male voice said from behind Dani.

Dani twisted in her seat, relieved to see Gavin standing barely a foot away.

"Aw, come on, Gav," the passenger—Shane, apparently—said, chuckling softly. "We were just having some fun."

"Yeah," Gavin said, "looks like a real blast." He made the faintest shooing motion. "Now get out of here."

"Whatever, man." Shane sniffed, but his buddy was already backing away. "See you later, ladies," he said, letting his tongue hang out obscenely before wandering off with his less aggressive friend.

"Um, thanks, Gavin," Zoe said, the hard edge to her voice gone and a blush creeping up her neck. "Would you like to—"

"Enjoy your dinner," Gavin said, then headed for the bar.

"Sigh," Dani said, following his path with her eyes. Absent-mindedly, she picked up a fry to nibble on.

“Seriously,” Zoe breathed.

Gavin sat at the lone barstool that had opened up, ordered a drink, and pulled out his cell phone, bringing it up to his ear.

“Who do you think he’s talking to?” Dani asked.

“His mom,” Zoe said definitively. “Or his grandma.”

“Definitely not his girlfriend,” Dani added, “because he doesn’t have one.”

“Damn straight,” Zoe said, taking a swig of her beer. “When he gets off that phone…”

“What? You’re going to make him an offer he can’t refuse?” Dani said, giggling and shimmying her shoulders.

Zoe threw her head back and laughed fully. “If I didn’t know any better, I’d think you’re calling me a slut.”

“A perpetual flirt,” Dani said. “You just can’t help yourself.” Zoe wasn’t a saint, by any means, but she wasn’t easy, either. Dani often thought that Jason had a lot to do with that. The only time Zoe’s brother acted like he cared what happened to his little sister was when it came to guys, so Zoe had grown used to using them to get back at Jason and piss him off. Flirting was a natural side effect, something Dani wasn’t sure her friend could ever fully turn off.

Maybe five minutes passed, and Gavin lowered the phone, tucking it back into his pocket. He shot a quick glance over his shoulder, almost like he was checking to see if Dani and Zoe were still there, then faced forward to nurse his beer.

“Alright,” Zoe said, gulping down the final quarter of her beer. She’d yet to even touch her burger and fries. “Wish me luck.” Like she ever needed it.

“Go get ’em, tiger,” Dani said, saluting Zoe with her cider glass.

Zoe stood and squared her shoulders, then marched straight over to Gavin. There was a decent enough gap on his left side between his stool and the next, and Zoe didn’t hesitate to wedge herself into the space, resting her elbow on the bar and signaling the bartender. She touched Gavin's arm and said something Dani couldn't hear over the ruckus filling the bar.

Dani took a gulp of cider, then another, thinking that maybe this brand of liquid courage was what she needed to finally confess the truth to Zoe. "I'm leaving for college," she said, practicing to Zoe's empty seat. She cleared her throat and sat up straighter. "I'm leaving," she repeated, then exhaled, wilting in her chair and taking another drink.

When Dani glanced back at the bar, Zoe's body language had changed dramatically. She'd stiffened and was leaning away from Gavin, almost to the effect of sitting on the lap of the guy behind her. Not that he seemed to mind.

The bartender placed two pint glasses on the bar, and Zoe picked them up and made a seemingly casual retreat.

"What happened?" Dani asked, taking the fresh pint of cider from Zoe and setting it beside her still half-full glass. She wasn't sure she really needed the third, but since it was already sitting there…

Zoe sat in her chair with a huff and took a sip of beer before setting her glass on the table. She brushed a few flyaways out of her face and met Dani's eyes. "He invited us to stay at his house while he works on your car."

Dani's mouth fell open. Unbelievable.

"He doesn't trust Shane and his band of dickwads not to hassle us at the campsite." She cleared her throat. "His *wife*, Agatha, is making up the guest room for us." Zoe smiled, tight-lipped and bitter. "Apparently, she's eager for the company, since she usually works from home and all." She touched her hand to her forehead, then fanned her face. "That was so close."

Dani tried to hold in her amusement, she really did. But the situation was just so ridiculous she couldn't help it, and laughter bubbled up from her chest.

"I'm glad my discomfort amuses you." But even as it was clear that Zoe was trying to maintain her stern expression, cracks appeared in the facade, and soon she was laughing just as hard as Dani was.

When Dani's giggle fit finally waned, she wiped the tears of mirth from under her eyes and exhaled heavily. "One day, Zo, you'll find the broody fella of your dreams." She suppressed a convulsive giggle. "But today, my friend, is not that day."

"Dude, Gavin's got it made," Dani said, staring up at the clear night sky from her lounge chair. The moon was barely a sliver, and the stars were out in full force, bathing the world in a sense of wonder. Nothing bad could happen under a sky like this.

"Mm-hmm," Zoe murmured from the lounge chair beside Dani's. "I would totally marry Aggy if he hadn't already."

"Word."

Gavin's wife was, well, awesome. She was quietly gorgeous, and she was an artist, and apparently her work was popular enough to afford an amazing oceanfront home with a badass deck overlooking the Pacific Ocean, fully equipped with a hot tub and an array of seating.

Dani tore her gaze from the brilliant stars to glance at Zoe, just for a moment. "You should ask Aggy for some tips on how to break into the art world." Dani hesitated for a moment, then said, "Maybe see how the art scene is up in Seattle…" She inhaled deeply, holding her breath.

Dani could feel Zoe's eyes on the side of her face. "Why would I—" Zoe's question cut off with a soft, breathy laugh. "Seattle. So that's why you've been acting so manic lately—you decided to go to school there, didn't you?" She shook her head slowly. "I knew it was something."

Dani blew out her breath. "Are you mad?" She turned her head to look at Zoe, heart pounding in her chest.

Zoe extended her arm across the space between their reclining patio chairs, offering her hand to Dani.

Hesitantly, Dani placed her hand in Zoe's.

"Of course I'm not mad," Zoe said, giving Dani's hand a squeeze. "I am sad, though. I'll miss you pretty much all the time."

"I know, Zo." Dani blinked away tears. "This was the hardest decision I've ever had to make." A moment later, she added, "What if it's the wrong one?"

Zoe let out another soft laugh. "It's not."

"How do you know?"

Zoe offered her a tight smile. "I just do."

8

OCTOBER 25, 2 AE

Like most Mondays, today I worked with Jason on some of the archive projects we have going. Unlike most Mondays, today we worked in our new office behind the cottage. Jason, Biggs, and Jake were the masterminds behind it, with Becca's urging, of course. She's been wanting our boxes out of her dining room for months now. Alas, her wish has been granted. We're moved in, now, though most of our blueprints and guidebook materials and all of my sketching supplies are still in boxes, waiting to be organized in the adjoining archive room.

And, I'm not sure if it was the sound of the rain hitting the roof or the companionable silence Jason and I worked in as he helped me whittle away at my handbook project, but out of nowhere, it hit me. Jason and I are friends. Yes, we're siblings—we've always been that—but we've never been friends. Never have I known my brother the way I do now, after The Ending. We've been working side by side the past ten months with a mutual respect I never thought possible, until now. It seems idiotic when I think about it—how strange it is to be happy that I finally have a good relationship with my brother. How silly it is that we had such a crappy relationship before.

It's a strange realization to make, let alone write down. But that's what I do these days—write, decipher, record. And while I promised Jason I wouldn't include anything in the handbook about him without him knowing it, my journal is another matter entirely. It's mine. It's private. And, because the softer side of Jason is rarely seen by many, it struck me that I wanted to remember this part of him. Always.

"Just accept it, Dad," Jason yelled as he stalked toward the front door. "I'm in the fucking Army. It's done, so drop it." He shoved his feet into his running shoes and yanked the door open, pushing the screen door out with enough force that it bounced back at him, smacking his shoulder. He hardly noticed and was far from caring.

Hands balled into fists, Jason jogged down the porch stairs with a *thunk*, *thunk*, *thunk*. He'd barely been back from basic training for a day and his dad was already riding his ass about his decision to join the Army—more specifically, that Jason's decision was *wrong*. His dad claimed that it wasn't too late. That Jason could still back out. The conversation, which had already been headed south, took a nose dive when Jason told his dad it would be great if, for once in his life, he could be "even remotely fucking patriotic."

Jason launched into a fast run as soon as the soles of his shoes touched asphalt. The briny coastal air always did wonders to clear his head after one of the famed blowouts with his dad. Back in his high school days, the arguments had happened so often that fighting became the norm in the Cartwright house. His only consolation this time was that Zoe hadn't been there to witness the shouting match. Or, even worse, Dani.

Jason was only a couple minutes into the run and he was already sweating. It was warmer than usual for a late September evening in Bodega Bay. It would be cooler closer to the water.

Over the years, the breeze that came in off the Pacific Ocean had come to feel like a reliable old friend talking Jason down on his steam-blowing runs, and the extra exertion from running on the sand would burn through his excess anger and frustration more quickly than running on the road. He changed course, sprinting across the street before the upcoming intersection and heading toward Bodega Dunes Beach, a several-mile stretch of sandy beach northwest of town.

Jason had always been athletic—the myriad of sports he'd participated in since childhood kept him in good shape—but basic training had pushed him to the next level. His body felt like a well-oiled, perfectly honed machine. Running was still as exhausting as ever, but it was now exhilarating, too.

Day was inching into dusk by the time Jason reached the beach, and gray smoke and the faint orange light of flames were visible a mile or two up the shore. Bonfires, a dozen of them from the looks of it. He figured it must be the high school kids, taking advantage of a Friday night the best way folks from Bodega Bay knew how—with a big-ass beach party. It was the only time all of the high schoolers came together, no matter their age or class.

Jason had been eager to leave his sleepy hometown behind, but the weekly parties on the beach during the summer were one of the few things he actually missed about this place. The tension at home and his never-ending fights with his dad, however…not so much. He already couldn't wait until his leave was over and he could get the hell away from this place. His home.

Picking up the pace, Jason pushed himself hard, heading straight for the glow of the fires. There were people he looked forward to seeing—old teammates who were a year behind him. Old girlfriends. He figured it best to burn off all of his excess anger and adrenaline before he reached them.

Jason slowed to a walk to cool down a little ways out, lifting the hem of his t-shirt to wipe his face and giving himself a sniff. He smelled like he'd been working hard, but he didn't stink. Good enough. He was more than a little sweaty, but the cool ocean air remedied that quickly enough. The faint sound of music was audible now, mostly just a baseline accompanied by the hum of voices and bursts of laughter from the partygoers.

As he drew near the revelry, Jason cracked his neck and inhaled and exhaled deeply. He was nervous, surprisingly, to the degree that he considered turning around and heading back down the beach. He felt like an outsider now, like he didn't belong to this place and these people anymore. That odd feeling convinced him to continue onward. His drive to tackle internal weaknesses was what had made him such a great athlete and what would, he hoped, make him a great soldier, too.

A group of girls he didn't recognize giggled as he passed their cluster on the outskirts of the party. They whispered to one another, one voicing Jason's name just loud enough for his ears to pick up. He could feel their eyes following him. *That* was one thing he didn't miss about this place.

"Well, if it isn't Captain America himself, gracing us lowly high schoolers with his presence." A stocky Asian guy strolled around the nearest bonfire.

Jason altered his trajectory to meet his old teammate. "Max," he said, laughing and holding his arms out. The two bro-hugged, patting each other on the back twice, then separated. "How the hell are you, man?"

"I'm doing alright, Cap," Max said, calling Jason by his old high school nickname like no time had passed at all. It surprised Jason to realize that it had only been a few months since he graduated from high school, despite him feeling like a totally different person now. Like that nickname didn't fit him anymore.

"How's the team this year?" Jason asked.

Max laughed wryly. "Honestly, we're struggling a bit. I'm trying to fill your shoes, but it's not easy following up the greatest quarterback our school's ever had."

"Nah." Jason thumped Max's shoulder. "You'll find your stride."

Max shrugged, expression none too sure. "I do what I can, I'll promise you that. Want a brew?" He nodded to a cluster of teenagers tucked under a rocky outcropping about thirty feet up shore.

"You know it," Jason said, falling into stride beside Max.

"I'm glad you came, man. I was starting to think you weren't going to show." Max pushed his way through the thirsty throng and emerged with two tall cans of Icehouse. "Your sister's been here for hours."

Jason had been about to tell Max that he hadn't even known about the party, but his comment was waylaid by the information about his sister. "Zoe's here?" He accepted the can of beer, eyes narrowing. She was still a kid, way too young for this shit. She was barely into her freshman year of high school, for fuck's sake. "Where is she?"

"Last time I saw her, she and Dani were over there," Max said, pointing to a bonfire closer to the water, about a football field away. "They're hanging out with a couple freshman guys."

Jason gripped his unopened can of beer, anger reigniting. "Which guys?"

"Glenn's kid brother and some shithead named Matt."

"Glenn's brother is a fucking delinquent," Jason said, scanning the silhouettes in Zoe and Dani's direction. A lick of flame highlighted the fiery red hair of a petite girl sitting on some kid's lap. Jason handed Max his unopened beer and headed that way before he had any kind of plan of what he was about to do.

Dani popped up to her feet when Jason was maybe ten paces away. When he was five paces away, Zoe rushed forward, stepping in front of Dani.

"You need to go home," Jason said, planting himself in front of his sister, arms crossed over his chest and jaw set.

Zoe mirrored him, one eyebrow raised. "No, Jason, I really don't."

"You two shouldn't be here." Jason's hard stare found Dani, standing a couple feet behind Zoe, arms hugging her middle and eyes opened wide. "You're too young for this shit."

The kid whose lap Dani had vacated—the one who had to be Glenn's little brother—stepped forward. "Come on, man. We're just—" His words died at a single glance from Jason. He raised his hands as though surrendering and backed away to stand with his little buddy and send sulky glares Jason's way.

"You shouldn't be hanging around these assholes," Jason said, uncrossing his arms and flicking a hand toward the two guys. "You shouldn't be down here to begin with. It's dangerous. What were you two thinking?" He laughed bitterly, focusing on Dani. "I thought you, at least, were smarter than this."

Dani's grip on her middle tightened, and her chin quivered. The moment the first tear emerged, Jason felt an unexpected tug in his chest. He hated making her cry, but this was for her own good. She was just a kid, and it was clear that Tweedle Dee and Tweedle Dipshit over there were more than willing to take advantage of her innocence.

Zoe glanced over her shoulder at Dani, and when she returned her attention to Jason, her eyes were narrowed into a vicious glare. "Why do you always have to be such a dick?"

Jason recrossed his arms.

Zoe stepped forward, shoving Jason so hard that he stumbled backward a couple steps. "Leave us alone, Jason. Just walk away. Leaving's what you do best, after all." She let that jab sink in for a moment. "We don't need you to watch over us. We do just fine on our own, no thanks to you." She recrossed her arms, glare hard. "So fuck off."

Jason returned Zoe's glare for a second longer, but he couldn't hold it. His anger was no longer directed at her, but at himself. He'd left—to join the Army, to get away from his dad, to escape the memories that haunted him whenever he looked at Zoe. It didn't matter the reason; it was clear that in Zoe's mind, he'd abandoned her. Maybe he had, but he'd done what he had to do to stay sane. To survive.

Shaking his head, Jason turned his back to his sister and walked away. One day, he would make it up to her. Not today.

"That looked intense, man," Max said, cracking open Jason's beer and returning it to him.

Jason brought the can up to his mouth and took a long drink, emptying a third of the can before lowering it and breathing deeply through his nose. "Fucking family," Jason said with a bitter laugh, his stare straying back to Zoe and Dani.

Max tapped his beer can against Jason's. "Amen."

Hours passed, and Jason found himself slowly surrounded by more and more teenagers from his old high school. Guys wanted to talk sports and hear about boot camp, and girls gave him puppy-dog eyes and sighed, asking him if and when he would be deployed, where he would have to go, and if he was afraid.

He eventually migrated to the central bonfire and settled in beside Max on a long piece of driftwood, since the bonfires on the outskirts of the party seemed reserved for those with more amorous intentions. Any other time, he would've been seeking out a companion to join him around one of those fires, but tonight, his gaze kept wandering back to Zoe and Dani. He felt the need to keep an eye on them, whatever claims his sister had made about them being able to look out for themselves. He didn't trust Glenn's dipshit of a brother, and he hated how handsy he'd been with Dani.

"And so Coach got all up in Gill's face, and…" Max was relaying some story about Coach Markle's latest post-loss inspirational bludgeoning, and Jason was only half listening. He responded with grunts and nods when appropriate, his attention on Dani, who was emphatically telling some story or something to Zoe and the little cluster of freshmen guys around their bonfire.

She was so bright and full of life now, not shut down and withdrawn like she'd been earlier, during Jason's scolding.

Zoe stood, smacked Dani's butt with the back of her hand—earning a squeal that even Jason could hear from fifty yards away—and started up the beach, heading in Jason's general direction. Dani said something to the guys, then skipped after Zoe to catch up. Zoe glanced at Jason as she passed him, her hard expression daring him to say something more, but Dani avoided looking his way.

He held his tongue.

A minute later, Zoe passed him again, a bottle of some chick drink in hand. She was alone, this time, and she ignored him. When she reached her bonfire, she held her hand out to one of the boys, pulling him up and guiding him around to the far side of the fire. Jason could've sworn she shot one last glance his way before disappearing behind the roaring flames.

Jason clenched his jaw and narrowed his eyes. She was testing him, he knew that. But fuck it, he couldn't just sit there while his sister did God knows what with some guy just to prove a point. "Be right back, man," he said to Max, standing.

He got three steps in before Dani ambushed him. "Hey," she said, handing him a beer. She hung onto what appeared to be a wine cooler for herself. She peered around, seeming to avoid looking at him, like more than a second or two of eye contact pained her. "I, um…" She cleared her throat and licked her lips. "I just wanted to say, um, thanks…for caring, I mean."

Jason raised his eyebrows.

"Zoe's just…" Dani lifted one shoulder, then let it fall. "I don't know. She's overwhelmed…with your dad and everything, you know? She didn't mean what she said down there. We don't—she doesn't want you to leave again, and she knows you have to." Dani offered him a closemouthed smile, finally meeting his eyes for more than a fleeting moment. "I, um, just wanted you to know."

With that, she turned to start back down toward her waiting admirers.

Jason reacted without thinking. He grabbed her arm, halting her retreat. The thought of Zoe down there with some freshman scumbag bothered him, but the idea of Dani ending up in the same position as his sister spurred a sense of revulsion so intense that he wanted to keep her nearby—keep her safe—no matter what. "Come on," he said, nodding to his momentarily abandoned driftwood. "Sit with me. Tell me more about what's been going on around here since I left."

Dani's eyes widened, the green of her irises flashing emerald in the firelight. "Really?"

Jason's lips widened into his first genuine smile of the evening.

Max seemed to read some unspoken and unconscious cue from Jason, because he was up and walking away before Jason and Dani even sat down.

Dani scoffed as she lowered herself down onto the driftwood beside Jason. "Nothing nearly as exciting as what's been going on with you, I'm sure." She was quiet for a moment, turning her wine cooler around and around in her hand. "Oh!" She perked up. "I got a job at the Riders' Ranch, so I'm finally making headway with the car fund. I should be able to afford something in, oh, say…" She scrunched up her nose, laughing at herself. "Three years or so."

Jason raised his beer can to his mouth and took a sip. "Just in time for your escape from this place," he said dryly.

Dani looked at him, pure puzzlement written all over her face. "Why would I leave?" She looked at the fire. "I love it here. I love the people here and the smell of the ocean and the sound of the seagulls and the way the fog rolls in like it's coming home." She glanced at Jason. "Besides, I wouldn't want to leave Grams."

Jason realized he was staring at the side of her face, captivated by her love of this place—their home—and he forced himself to avert his gaze to the flames. "That makes sense."

"So…" Dani turned on the driftwood, raising one leg and

tucking the foot under the other, all bubbling energy again. “What was it like?”

Jason looked at her. “What?”

She smacked his arm. “Army training, you dork. Was it hard? Did they yell at you? Or make you cry? Or did anyone beat you with a soap in a sock?”

Jason chuckled. “Yes, yes, no, and no, thankfully.”

Dani bit her lip, eyebrows drawing together. “Do you know what happens to you next?”

Jason returned his focus to the fire, his beer dangling from his fingertips between his knees. “I get assigned to a base, leave for there in a few days, and then, eventually, I get deployed…to Iraq or Afghanistan or somewhere else. I won’t know until I know.” Jason could feel Dani’s gaze on him, but neither said anything for long seconds. The crackle of the fire filled the silence between them, accompanied by the gentle crash of waves, the muted music, and the chatter and laughter of the teenagers all around them on the beach.

“Are you afraid?” Dani finally asked.

And for the first time that night—for the first time ever—Jason felt compelled not to just shrug that question off like it was no big deal. He wanted to answer, to confide in someone. He wanted to confide in Dani.

He looked at her, just met her eyes for a moment, taking in the concern and maybe even fear she felt for him. She wasn’t trying to hide her emotions, so for once, he thought he might be able to risk emotional honesty, too. For once, he might be brave, like her.

“Yeah,” he whispered. “I’m terrified.”

9

JANUARY 30, 3 AE

It's becoming pretty clear that something's off with Becca. For a while now, she's been distant and absentminded, not to mention that she keeps slipping off to somewhere and we don't see her for hours. Jake and Gabe think it's her growing affection for Austin, our New Bodega ambassador, but I know it's something else, I can feel it. She's never as easy to read as the rest—it's a Re-gen thing—but I've been struggling to pry into that vaulted mind of hers. Despite the difficulty, a sickening feeling won't let me ignore it.

And I think I finally know what's going on with her. Last night, I had a dream—her dream, I'm fairly certain—like the time I saw her prophecy of Jason at the Colony with our mom. It was the only truth we had during his disappearance, the only clue to know he was still alive and where we would find him. But this time, I've seen the terrifying secret Becca has been keeping from us. I can barely fathom it, let alone find the words to describe it.

Things are changing. The future of humankind is so uncertain, tears burn my eyes. I have to write it down—get it out of me, somehow—even if I can't tell anyone. I need to find Becca so she can explain what it is I saw. I need her to explain the insanity I witnessed.

In the dream, I saw—

AFTERWORD

HARVEST, 285 AE

Reading the final words in Zoe's journal sent a chill down my spine. What had she been about to write? What had she seen?

I can't help but wonder if it was *us*, now, in this time and place that is so different from hers. It seems fated that I would find her journal, like she was writing specifically to me, so that I would know what her world was really like—so different from what we're told. And now, of all possible moments, to discover that *they* were like us. That Zoe was like me. That she was a person. A human being with fears and memories and so many secrets.

Her journal has changed my entire perception of the world, only leaving me more curious, more desperate to uncover the truth.

Because of her, I'm determined to do so.

Be sure to read *World After*, the prequel to The Ending Legacy.

MORE BOOKS BY THE LINDSEYS

THE ENDING WORLD

THE ENDING LEGACY
World After (Prequel)
The Raven Queen

THE ENDING SERIES
After The Ending
Into The Fire
Out Of The Ashes
Before The Dawn
The Ending Beginnings
World Before

SAVAGE NORTH CHRONICLES
(by Lindsey Pogue)

The Darkest Winter
The Longest Night
Midnight Sun
Fading Shadows
Untamed
Unbroken
Day Zero: Beginnings

ALSO BY LINDSEY POGUE

FORGOTTEN LANDS WORLD
(Can be read as stand-alones)

FORGOTTEN LANDS
Dust and Shadow
Borne of Sand and Scorn (Prequel)
Earth and Ember
Tide and Tempest

RUINED LANDS
City of Ruin
Sea of Storms
Land of Fury

SARATOGA FALLS LOVE STORIES
(Recommended reading order)
Whatever It Takes
Nothing But Trouble
Told You So
Memory Book Story Collection

ALSO BY LINDSEY SPARKS

ECHO WORLD

ECHO TRILOGY

Echo in Time

Resonance

Time Anomaly

Dissonance

Ricochet Through Time

KAT DUBOIS CHRONICLES

Ink Witch

Outcast

Underground

Soul Eater

Judgement

Afterlife

FATELESS TRILOGY

Song of Scarabs and Fallen Stars

Darkness Between the Stars

THE NIK CHRONICLES

(Patreon exclusive serial)

LEGACIES OF OLYMPUS

ATLANTIS LEGACY

Sacrifice of the Sinners

Legacy of the Lost

Fate of the Fallen

Dreams of the Damned

Song of the Soulless

Blood of the Broken

Rise of the Revenants

ALLWORLD ONLINE

AO: Pride & Prejudice

AO: The Wonderful Wizard of Oz

Vertigo

AO: LOOKING GLASS

(Patreon exclusive serial)

THE LAST

VAMPIRE QUEEN

(Patreon exclusive serial)

Season 1: Awakened

ABOUT LINDSEY POGUE

Lindsey Pogue is a genre-bending fiction author, best known for her soul-stirring, post-apocalyptic survival series, Savage North Chronicles and Forgotten Lands. As an avid romance reader with a master's in history and culture, Lindsey's adventures cross genres and push boundaries, weaving together facts, fantasy, and timeless love stories of epic proportions. When Lindsey's not chatting with readers, plotting her next storyline, or dreaming up new, brooding characters, she's generally wrapped in blankets watching her favorite action flicks with her own leading man. They live in Northern California with their rescue cats, Beast and little girl Blue.

Access VIP Vault Exclusive stories, audiobooks, and more!
www.lindseypogue.com/newsletter

PATREON: https://www.patreon.com/lindseypogue
LINKTREE: https://linktr.ee/authorlindseypogue

MAIN SOCIAL MEDIA

FB Reader Group: Lindsey Pogue Reader Group
TikTok: @authorlindseypogue
Instagram: @authorlindseypogue
YouTube: Lindsey Pogue

OTHER SOCIAL MEDIA

Facebook: @authorlindseypogue
Pinterest: @authorlindseypogue

ABOUT LINDSEY SPARKS

Lindsey Sparks lives her life with one foot in a book—so long as that book transports her to a magical world or bends the rules of science. Her novels, from Post-apocalyptic (writing as Lindsey Fairleigh) to Time Travel Romance, always offer up a hearty dose of unreality, along with plenty of history, intrigue, adventure, and romance.

When she's not working on her next novel, Lindsey spends her time hanging out with her two little boys, working in her garden, or playing board games with her husband. She lives in the Pacific Northwest with her family and their small pack of cats and dogs. www.authorlindseysparks.com

PATREON: https://www.patreon.com/lindseysparks

MAIN SOCIAL MEDIA

Instagram: @authorlindseysparks
YouTube: Author Lindsey Sparks
Discord: discord.gg/smTeDHQBhT

OTHER SOCIAL MEDIA

TikTok: @authorlindseysparks
Pinterest: @authorlindseysparks

www.authorlindseysparks.com/join-newsletter

www.ingramcontent.com/pod-product-compliance
Lightning Source LLC
Chambersburg PA
CBHW070458170726
48291CB00008B/2566

* 9 7 8 1 9 4 9 4 8 5 0 5 9 *